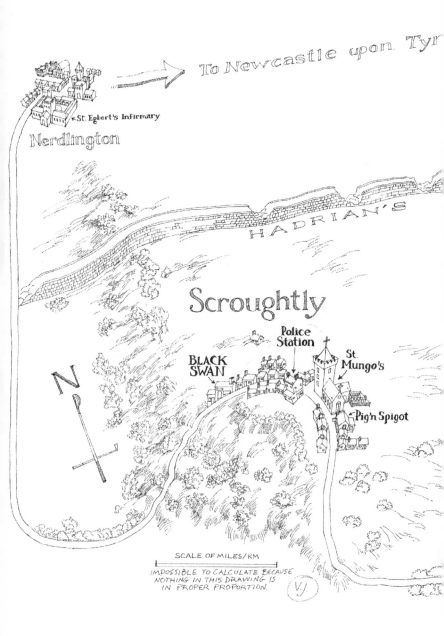

To Newcastle upon Tyr

Nerdlington

St. Egbert's Infirmary

HADRIAN'S

Scroughtly

BLACK SWAN

Police Station

St. Mungo's

Pig'n Spigot

N

SCALE OF MILES/KM

IMPOSSIBLE TO CALCULATE BECAUSE
NOTHING IN THIS DRAWING IS
IN PROPER PROPORTION.

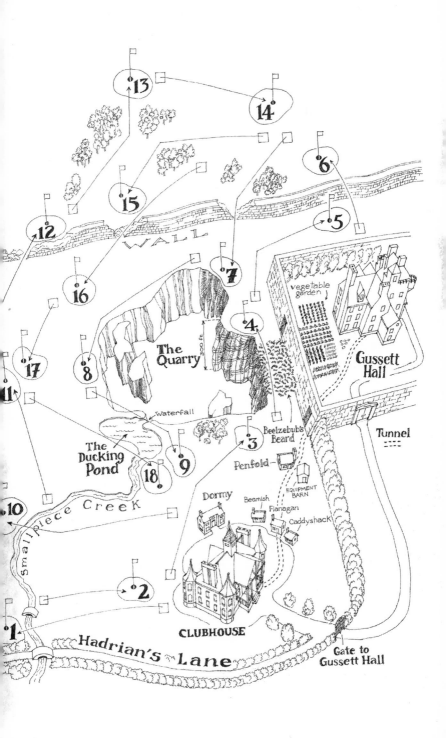

A NASTY BIT OF ROUGH

DAVID FEHERTY

BLACK IRISH ENTERTAINMENT LLC

LOS ANGELES　　**NEW YORK**

BLACK IRISH ENTERTAINMENT LLC
65 CENTRAL PARK WEST
NEW YORK, NY 10023

COPYRIGHT © 2002 BY DAVID FEHERTY
BOOK INTERIOR DESIGN BY BETH EAKIN
ART DIRECTION BY HSU AND ASSOCIATES
COVER ARTWORK, ENDPAPER ARTWORK, AND
INTERIOR ILLUSTRATIONS BY VICTOR JUHASZ

FIRST BLACK IRISH ENTERTAINMENT EDITION MAY 2013

FOR INFORMATION ABOUT SPECIAL DISCOUNTS FOR BULK PURCHASES
PLEASE VISIT WWW.BLACKIRISHBOOKS.COM

TRADE PAPERBACK ISBN: 978-1936891122

EBOOK ISBN: 978-936891-09-2

ALSO BY DAVID FEHERTY

NONFICTION

Somewhere in Ireland, a Village is Missing an Idiot
David Feherty's Totally Subjective History of the Ryder Cup
An Idiot for All Seasons
The Power of Positive Idiocy

FOR ANITA,

ALWAYS & FOREVER

PREFACE

T he beginning of this story will be familiar to some readers of *Golf Magazine*, in which three articles about Scrought's Wood and its collection of madcap members have already been published. However, a couple of years have passed since the last related article appeared in the magazine, so I hope you will forgive me if I spend a little while at the start of the book, recapping for those who are unfamiliar with the club's history.

Scrought's Wood Golf Club is in the county of Northumberland, near the village of Scroughtly. The course lies hidden in a deep cleft in the moors and is all but invisible, except from the air. The surrounding land extends north to Hadrian's Wall, the ancient border between Scotland and England, and is owned by Major General (retired) Sir Richard Gussett, who is also the club chairman. To all, he is known simply as "Uncle Dickie." Most of the members, staff, and caddies are associated with Uncle Dickie through military service, having served either under or alongside him in various campaigns throughout the world.

Some are disabled men who could not have found employment elsewhere, some are men that society has rejected because they have chosen to be different, and others are simply old friends who share Uncle Dickie's philosophy. The way of life the club affords them protects them from an intolerant and judgmental outside world, and all of the club's characters are united in a common love and respect for Uncle Dickie. They are also united in the belief that their golf club was the first ever, and is the birthplace of the game.

The following is the story of the Scrought's Wood Golf Club and its longstanding rivalry with the McGregor clan, of the Tay Club, who claim that it was *their* ancestors who invented the game many centuries ago. The McGregors have a three-hole golf course that stretches for four and a half miles along the northern shore of the Firth of Tay, and twice every century, armed with the tools of the game, both ancient and modern, they do battle with the members of Scrought's Wood. The prize is the oldest trophy in golf, the petrified middle finger of St. Andrew, known simply as "The Digit." For Uncle Dickie, the old soldier, this is perhaps his last chance to do battle, and even the scorecard on a miscarriage of justice that took place fifty years ago. For the members there is more than some fossilized human remains at stake.

It is a rivalry between North and South that has lasted for centuries, during which time each side has had its share of both villains and heroes. In golf, cowardice is a furtive kick, and a man's courage has always been measured by his honesty, even in the face of a painful defeat. This is the game the way Uncle Dickie plays it and his play provides an open window to his soul.

This book is about people who oppose each other, in more ways than one. It is about greed and envy, hatred and tolerance, love and stupidity (quite a lot of stupidity, actually). But most of all, it is a story about the faith that real friends have in one another and how that faith is never wasted, so long as at least one of them holds on to it.

We live in a world where athletes, clergymen, musicians, and politicians are considered to be important, even heroic at times. For Uncle Dickie, no one is more important than a child, a nurse, a teacher, or a forgotten soldier. I hope you enjoy this book, and wherever you are, may you always have an Uncle Dickie who loves you.

William David Feherty

A NASTY BIT OF ROUGH

CHAPTER ONE

When I was a snot-nosed youth in Ireland, my father did everything in his power, as did my soon-to-be sainted mother, to steer me away from the travails of what possessed my Uncle Dickie, who lived across the water in England. When I was a wee lad, Uncle Dickie sat me on his knee, and regaled me with stories about the genesis of a game that involved trying to jam a ball into a hole in the ground with a stick, and how his and thence my ancestors had in fact invented it. Through the years, Uncle Dickie's passion became mine, and to the horror of my beloved parents, I too have made a life of mashies, niblicks, nudgers, and wassocks. As Uncle Dickie is still shooting below his age and is of sound mind and body, it is only fitting—nay, it is my duty—to tell the real truth about what befell him not so long ago.

Major General (retired) Sir Richard Gussett presides over the most exclusive golf course in the world, a club so secretive that its whereabouts are unknown to all but a select few. In fact, some of its members have a hard time finding it.

Scrought's Wood refused the British Royal charter back in the 1850s, citing the fact that they wouldn't want to be associated with people who behaved like royalty—a move, which, while it seemed like madness at the time, now looks prophetic, to say the least. They also refused to have anything to do with the Royal and Ancient Golf Club of St. Andrews, believing that Scrought's Wood is the birthplace of the game, and its members the true guardians of the Rules of Golf.

No new members have been accepted into the club since 1960 and, due to attrition, only nine remain. Most of these men are veterans of the First and Second World Wars, in which they served King and country, fighting under Sir Dickie's command.

It is believed that the golf club was founded back in 1321 by a Franciscan monk known as Brother Dick, a profoundly devout but unbalanced character, who believed he had been commanded by God to impregnate as many of the local village's virgins as he possibly could. In between these fits of righteous fornication, he passed the time by playing a solitary game of his own invention, high up on the moors.

The object of his game was to hit a ball, fashioned from a badger's testicle stuffed with gannet feathers, with a variety of sticks until it fell into a hole in the ground, in as few strokes as possible. Local legend has it that Brother Dick was often seen on the windswept hilltops, silhouetted against the darkening sky with his long flowing robes flapping behind him. He was a frightening figure, flailing away with his shepherd's crook, intermittently screaming obscenities and shaking his fists at the heavens, then falling to his knees in tearful supplication. A few yards behind him trudged a small, hunched figure, carrying what must have looked like a bag of branches. After each of these soul-searching blasphemous journeys across the moors with his strange collection of wooden sticks, Brother Dick would return to a small room in the monastery and faithfully make an entry in a primitive scorecard-journal:

This morning, after I did sow the seed of the Lord into the furrow of Ethel, daughter of Eldrick the Unbearable, my thoughts turned once more to the second challenge the Holy Father has set for me. Stout was my heart, and glorious was my swing, as my beloved servant, "John the Turnip," and I manfully strode out across the sacred ground. Great and mighty joy did I feel when across the heather, the bollock I smote in just four great cuts. But alas, once more did the Lord deny me entry to the small pit that I have fashioned for his glorification, upon the grass of great shortness.

As always, with temptation did I struggle and to make greater the pit would surely have been the easier path. But the voice of the sweet and merciful Lord, whose wisdom knows no limitation, held me back and directed me instead to deal with my staff, a mighty blow to the sack of John, who is without question, the worst branch-holder in all of God's creation. In this I found some comfort. May the Lord have mercy upon the wobbly bits of his manhood, and teach the filthy, rotten bastard what is the difference between a nudger and a sharp-ended wassock. I mean, really!

So anyway, Lord, another bastard of a six I did make, but thankful I am for your great mercy all the same. No matter that badgers are scarce and, at last count, I have forty-seven children aged four years or less. That is, if thou countest not Gertrude, daughter of Desmond the Disturbing, who is about to drop another squealer on me. But thank you, heavenly Father, for the blessings thou hast bestowed upon my unworthy self, and in thine infinite mercy, this one thing of thee I beg once more: If thou couldst possibly see thine own way clear to let me smite the bollock into the pit in four smites only. Thou art killing me here. Humbly, I beseech thee, grant this thy servant one four, lest he should toss his personal self from the walls of this place,

and into the pile of dung that lies below the refectory window.

The yellowing parchments that rest upon the shelves of the Great Library in Uncle Dickie's manor, Gussett Hall in Scroughtly, reveal to historians that the world's first golfer was a tortured soul indeed. Local legend has it that one rainy afternoon in the autumn of 1331, after nudging his bollock just wide of the pit for a four, Brother Dick calmly made his way back to his room, and made a final entry in his journal. Then he flung himself to his death from the ramparts of the castle that would later become the ancestral home of Sir Richard Gussett.

It read, " O Lord God, Forgive." In other words: O-L-G-F.

Some years later, the game was named by one of Brother Dick's fellow monks, who was apparently dyslexic.

Today, the criteria required for membership into Scrought's Wood are incredibly difficult to meet. They include a blood oath of secrecy, the ability to consume vast quantities of single malt Scotch, and if a member is married, that his spouse is probably under the impression that he died some years ago.

The club's one concession to modern technology at Scrought's Wood is a satellite dish—a necessity really, as the members worship the game like a religion and feel it their duty to record and review every broadcast of every event.

For instance, Uncle Dickie and his cronies were watching the U.S. Open a few years ago when the USGA ran its commercial, "We didn't give birth to the game, but we've been its legal guardian for the last one hundred years." That sent a few good swallows of Guinness out through noses and ruined a couple of magnificent handlebar mustaches.

Old-fashioned they may be, but unenlightened they are not, so

Uncle Dickie expressed his discomfort in a letter to me. As I live in the United States, where I masquerade as a television announcer, he besieged me to plead his case in the court of public opinion.

Davey, my boy,

So nice to hear from you and thank you for inquiring about your Auntie Myrtle. Seventy years old last week and the old boiler is still beautiful, and fit enough to drain a bottle of Bushmills with me in a single sitting, bless her sturdy support hose. She sends her love. Now to business, dear nephew. You are indeed correct to be worried about the latest ominous rumblings from the bowels of the United States Golf Association. As always, any change they make will be for the worse.

In the name of all that's right and drawing back to the fairway, just who the hell do they think they are? Don't they realize that there were only two Rules in the original game? Thou shalt play the ball as it lies, and Thou shalt play the course as thou findest it.

These two Rules gave birth to some of the greatest technological developments in the sport, all of which were totally necessary. These latest clubs are simply a part of the evolution of the game and must be protected at all costs. We have lost too much already.

Take, for instance, Hamish McShug's patented splatterguard niblick (circa 1835), which was rendered obsolete when the Royal Asses poked their noses in and deemed the cow pat an immovable obstruction. Of course, you and I know the cowpat is always immovable, especially when you are trying to get it out of your britches, hence Hamish's splatterguard.

Even then, if you let it dry and use a stiff brush, you're whistling Dixie, as they say over there in Yankee land.

But listen, young fellow, there may yet be a silver lining to this cloud of hot air.

Personally, I feel this latest attempt to halt the natural evolution of the game may result in something of a peasants' revolt, and perhaps we here at Scrought's Wood will finally have our say. Sanity may yet prevail.

There may be thirty-five clubs in my bag, but every one of them is necessary. Just say you find yourself in a wheel rut. Your standard niblick simply won't do the job to extricate it. Hence, we had the invention of the rutting iron.

Just imagine if we at the Wood took our rightful place as guardians of the sacred game. The Bible has but ten rules, so why the hell should a simple game have thirty-four, with a six-hundred-page book of decisions?

Here's our decisions book: Hit it and stop whining. That should speed up play. A golf course is a canvas, my boy, upon which the best and worst players may create their masterpieces. One must always remember: A low score is never an insult to the golf course, but rather a compliment to both the player and the hallowed ground upon which he walks.

Davey, we here at the Wood are delighted with your progress in the United States. Your broadcasting position serves us well by giving you the opportunity to make average golfers aware of how this sacred game should be played, despite what the so-called ruling bodies may say. I wouldn't trust them to rule a straight line. So, be vocal, dear boy, and make us proud. In twenty years' time, perhaps you will, as a member of the Holy Wood, take your seat upon the committee that will restore the game to its original glory. Or perhaps you will just take your seat in the snug and drool, like my dear

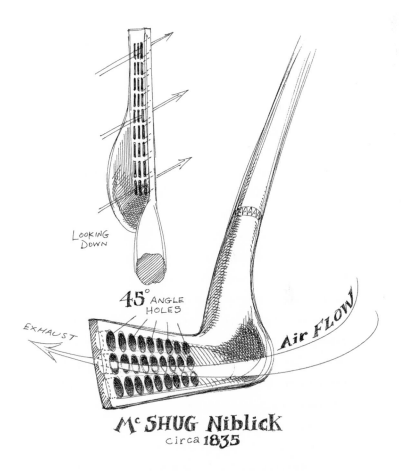

LOOKING DOWN

45° ANGLE HOLES

EXHAUST

Air FLOW

Mc SHUG Niblick
circa 1835

The Splatterguard Niblick (McShug, Hamish. *1835*).

Specifically designed for the "extrication of the ball from heavy mud, watery filth, dung piles, or other excrement."

A lowland farm boy from the coastal town of Ayr, McShug played his golf not on the links, but inland on the cattle pastures of local dairy farmers. This ingenious club was designed with exhaust ports to channel away any matter that might otherwise have found its way onto the clothing of the user, and was not normally found in the bags of the upper class, who had the privilege of playing on turf that was tightly nibbled by sheep, and considerably less messy.

old friend Bertie Featherstone. Sadly, Bertie popped his clogs two weeks ago. How I will miss our Wednesday night political arguments. His was the second death we've suffered in recent weeks, the first being our beloved greenskeeper, Penfold, whom you will no doubt remember as the "Sod Father." Penfold Jr. will carry on, of course. His father was planted in the staff plot behind the thirteenth green, and as is our custom here at Scrought's Wood, three bottles of thirty-year-old McCallan's single malt were poured over his grave. Naturally, we drank them first.

As for Squadron Leader Featherstone, we granted him his last wish, and had him stuffed and placed for all eternity upon his usual barstool in the snug. The taxidermist was initially a little vexed, but did a fine job with the old boy, rendering him cheerier of countenance than at any time during his living years. The only other noticeable differences are that he has stopped drooling, and he falls off the barstool considerably less often than he used to. Also, his breast pocket makes a frightfully good ashtray.

Well, that's the news for now, so toodle-pip, my boy, and don't be a stranger.

Always with love,
Gussett of the Wood

Needless to say, my cowardice about bringing up Uncle Dickie's polemic on the air may have saved me my position alongside McCord, but lately it has been wearing on me. But as they say, the pen is mightier than the sword. So, it is with honor that I present to you the whole truth of what valiant men like Uncle Dickie are up against in this world obsessed with rules. A testament, if you will, to a man devoted to a game, a club, and the necessity of having at least one enemy around in order to keep life interesting. So what follows is the absolutely almost true tale of my dear Uncle Dickie, his demonic match with the McGregor clan of Tay, and of how his most precious values were compromised. As Dear Uncle Dickie would say, "It was a nasty bit of rough, hard to pass, and harder to forget."

CHAPTER TWO

Uncle Dickie, lord of the manor, is the sprightliest seventy-eight-year-old you could possibly imagine. Every morning he does his exercises, dressed in a stout pair of brown leather walking shoes and calf-length black socks, with his string vest tucked securely into a pair of Y-fronts. Twenty push-ups, twenty deep-knee bends, twenty sit-ups, and five minutes skipping, followed by ten minutes of meditation in the lotus position. "Keeps a fellow stout of heart," he is fond of saying.

After this, he dresses in one of his many three-piece tweed suits, and finishes by waxing the tips of his trophy handlebar mustache. After a goodbye kiss to Myrtle, his beloved wife of fifty-two years, he tucks the *Daily Telegraph* under his arm and drives at high speed in his souped-up Bentley from Gussett Hall over to the club, where he has his breakfast of tea, toast, two poached eggs, and fried ham. Down the hallway, on his way to the bar, generally he stops for a moment to admire the displayable portion of his club collection—the best and most valuable in the entire world—some of which is housed in glass cases built into the walls.

Uncle Dickie can afford to spend much of his time at Scrought's Wood because he owns all of the land upon which Gussett Hall and Scrought's Wood were built. He is also the major landowner around the town of Scroughtly. Some of this vast and beautiful estate was left to him by his parents, Lord Waldo and Lady Emily Gussett, and the rest he acquired through brilliant transactions after the Second World War.

While this leaves him in a position to control virtually every aspect of the lives of the villagers, very few of them have the slightest reason to dislike him. On the contrary, he is the most beloved of the village's 150 residents.

You could call him a liberal-minded conservative. He is completely nondenominational, unprejudiced, and tolerant, as evidenced by the membership of Scrought's Wood. The cast of characters at the Wood includes Francis Hannigan, an Irish rabbi; Jahindir Poonsavvy, an Indian maharajah; Willoughby Hurd, an escapee from a nearby mental institution; Brigadier Spearman Kodogo, a Zulu; Reginald Carstairs, a former cat-burglar, now obese; Mickey Crutchlode, a monocled misanthrope; Major Norman Oglesby, an elderly ornithologist; Rear Admiral Sir Denis Boothely-Spifford; and a gaggle of gay, crippled, and insane caddies.

Uncle Dickie has always felt that other people have tried to stop the evolution of the game, and he is driven by his ambition to return it to its roots. He has stated on more than one occasion that he wishes his epitaph to be the most basic tenet of golf: Play the course as you find it, and the ball as it lies. If you need two caddies to carry all your clubs, so what? Manufacturers should be able to make whatever they want, and if you don't have a club to fit a particular situation, have one made. He refuses to acknowledge the existence of the Royal & Ancient and the USGA, the ruling bodies of the game in most of the world. The only authority in the game, Uncle Dickie says, is the conscience of the man who swings the club.

However, Scrought's Wood, despite its seemingly anachronistic nature, is not immune to the modern-day problems that crop up in our politically correct world. A man's race, religion, or sexual preference would never exclude him from membership, but the club had always been, by design, utterly devoid of females. Then, one day out of a clear blue sky, there loomed a huge, dark, feminine thundercloud.

Major Oglesby, the senile old codger, tried for years to get his son, Nigel—a member of the town council and an oxygen thief of the highest order—into the club, but naturally the membership would have none of it. For starters, he was only forty-seven years old and according to Uncle Dickie, "a raving pinko."

Uncle Dickie had told Oglesby on numerous occasions that there was more chance of his backside going snipe-shooting than the ghastly fruit of his loins ever becoming a member of the Wood. Nonetheless, Oglesby insisted on using the one-guest-per-decade rule to invite his chinless offspring out to play golf. Penfold Jr., Uncle Dickie's trusty greenskeeper, set up the course in exactly the same fashion that caused Walter Hagen to wet his plus-fours after fifteen holes in 1929, but still, Oglesby and his son made it back to the clubhouse uninjured.

That's when the trouble started. It was lunchtime and Dickie was sitting on his customary stool at the bar, sharing a yarn and a snifter with Admiral Boothely-Spifford, when in came Oglesby and his idiot child, who was trailing grass across the Persian from a pair of those infernal shoes without spikes. Dickie noticed, not without satisfaction, as they walked from the eighteenth green, that Dwilby, Agnes Flanagan's terrier, had attached himself to the junior Oglesby's leg. Half Jack Russell, half miniature schnauzer, Dwilby was a wild-eyed shaggy little mutt with a penchant for anything female or, for that matter, anything stationary. Given half a chance, the dog would shag the leg off the dining room table.

When they came in, to Uncle Dickie's amazement, the upstart Oglesby sat down heavily next to the bay window in Reggie Carstairs' chair and asked Crump, the wine steward, to bring him something that sounded like a "strawberry dackberry." No one knew what he was talking about; naturally, Crump ignored him. Then, on the stroke of 12:30, in came Carstairs who calmly walked over to where Oglesby the younger was seated, sat down heavily upon him, and began to read the *Daily Telegraph*.

Carstairs is not the smallest member at the Wood. In fact, Dickie's half a man Friday, Stanley Beamish, once remarked that he'd be considerably taller if he lay down, so you can imagine how uncomfortable the guest was, until his father arrived and asked Dickie if he'd seen Nigel.

"What sort of a name is Nigel, anyway, I ask you?" Dickie asked of the Admiral, who shrugged his shoulders.

"Yes, Oglesby, old chap," Uncle Dickie said. "I believe he's under the stairs!" At this stage, Nigel's frantically wiggling arms were the only things visible beneath the vast bulk of the chair's rightful occupant and by the time Major Oglesby had persuaded Carstairs to stand up, the man was navy blue and floppy.

Crump revived the little toad with a large brandy and that's when Nigel started his tirade. Once he got his breath back, he began yelling about elitism and sexist behavior, and for a moment Uncle Dickie thought he was trying to butter them up, but then he stormed out, shouting something about his lawyer. Even his father seemed relieved to see him go.

A couple of days later, Uncle Dickie did indeed receive a letter from Junior Oglesby's lawyer, threatening him with something called the Civil Liberties Act and stating that if he did not admit a female member, within thirty days the Wood could be subject to closure!

Uncle Dickie could not have been more shocked! He was immediately struck by images of curtains and throw pillows in the lounge.

"Nay, nay, and thrice nay," he shouted to no one in particular.

Uncle Dickie was on the telephone right away, placing calls to the House of Lords and to his legal counsel, Lord Knodes. Then he called an extraordinary general meeting of the membership. The news Knodes brought the members was dismaying, to say the least, as they learned that the local council had passed an equal opportunity ordinance that affected the entire county.

It seemed the obsequious Oglesby boy had them all over a barrel, and even his father admitted that the child was, indeed, "A skid mark on the underwear of England."

It was a desperate situation, and normally that is when those at the Wood rise to their very best. But this time, Uncle Dickie had to admit, he was stumped for an answer. There was nothing else for it.

He simply had to go and ask the one person whose advice he could always fall back on in times such as these— Auntie Myrtle. So, hoping to catch her between her afternoon nap and her early evening coughing fit, he hopped into the Bentley and set off for Gussett Hall.

As luck would have it, when he arrived she was having tea and crumpets in the conservatory. She noticed his grave expression, and immediately asked him what was wrong.

As Uncle Dickie used to say, "Auntie Myrtle might be one teat short of an udder most of the time, but in times of crisis she is still prone to the occasional blinding flash of lucidity." Luckily for the Wood, this was one such time.

He pursed his lips thoughtfully, placed a hand on his wife's knee, and said, "Myrtle, old girl, I don't know what the world is coming to, and I need your advice. It's bad enough that the game is going to the dogs, and we have a bunch of idiots devising new rules every other day, but now the Oglesby boy has initiated an attack, and it looks like the club may be done for if we don't admit a female member."

Aunt Myrtle put her teacup down and smiled at him. "Well, I'm not sure I can do anything about the rules, dear," she said, "but the solution to your most immediate problem would appear to be obvious."

Uncle Dickie stared at her blankly for a moment.

"Er, yes, my precious," he said awkwardly. "Let's just say for the moment that it's not exactly obvious to all of us."

"Oh, honestly Richard," Myrtle said. "There is always a solution, no matter how prickly the problem. In this case, if you and the boys insist on maintaining the status quo at the club, one of you will have to make the supreme sacrifice. Simple, really."

Uncle Dickie stood up abruptly, his mouth open in shock.

"Good Lord, Myrtle!" he exclaimed. "Of course!" He bent over, kissed her on the cheek, and then turned smartly on his heel and marched toward the door, slapping his palms together and rubbing them briskly, his mood suddenly lighter. "Thanks awfully, old girl."

So, armed with the obvious, Uncle Dickie hurried to the Bentley and headed at high speed back to Scrought's Wood, where, anxiously, the brethren awaited. As in the past, in times of great gravity, all members retired to the drawing room, took their assigned seats, and Crump dimmed the lights.

"Gentlemen," Dickie announced, "One of us must become a woman."

In any other golf club, a statement such as this might have caused uproar, but the members of the Wood were made of different stuff. The news Uncle Dickie brought was met with stoic silence, and complete calm.

Uncle Dickie motioned to Crump, who brought the straw box and set it down in front of him. As he was about to draw the first straw, Major Oglesby broke the silence.

"Ahem, I say, old chaps," he stammered. "I feel it only fair that we play a member match to settle the matter."

CHAPTER THREE

The floorboards under the worn carpet squeaked and complained, as Uncle Dickie strode purposefully down the corridor from his office to the locker room, where he sat down on a bench, opened his locker, and began to put on a pair of metal spiked, brown leather golf shoes. Moments later he was scrunching his way across the gravel toward the tenth tee, where the rest of the members were waiting. The caddies were in a small huddle behind the tee, deep in hushed conversation.

Herpy stood at the back of the group with a bag on each shoulder. Normally, he didn't say much, but the whole concept of this match was too much for him. His nickname had been acquired from Caddiemaster Seamus Flanagan who had said, "Most of the time you wouldn't know he was there, but every now and then, he can be an irritating dick head."

"Let me get this straight," Herpy said incredulously. "They're playing a match t'decide which one of them has to get a sex-change operation, right?"

Flanagan looked at Herpy, and then at the rest of the men.

"Exactly," he said, as if it were nothing out of the ordinary.

Thirsty McManus, Poonsavvy's looper, pursed his lips, and let out a low whistle, shaking his head.

Uncle Dickie stood on the back edge of the tee with his feet apart, and his hands clasped behind his back. "Right, boys," he exclaimed gravely. "We all know how serious this is, so let's get on with it. We will play as many holes as it takes, and this will be a survival match, with whoever scores the lowest on each hole being relieved. The rest will continue until only one man remains. That man will become a woman at his earliest convenience. Is that understood?"

The members nodded and mumbled their acceptance as Uncle Dickie unsheathed one of the many drivers in the two bags that hung from Flanagan's shoulders. He stretched, bent over to tee up his ball, gave a couple of waggles, and promptly topped his tee shot down the left half of the fairway.

"Oooh," he gasped, grabbing the small of his back. "I'm a little stiff."

Herpy looked sideways at Flanagan and hissed out of the corner of his mouth, "It might be the last time he gets a little stiff, if he hits any more like that 'un."

Mickey Crutchlode went next, hitting a nice little draw about two hundred yards out, and one by one the members followed. All of them hit the fairway except Major Oglesby, who hit a violent snap hook into the left rough just before the ninesome made its way down the fairway.

Uncle Dickie was the first to reach his tee shot, and had about 250 yards to the front of the green.

"Playing long today, Flanagan," he muttered as he set up over the ball with a metal 3-wood, and made an elegant swing, sending the ball shooting low toward the right edge of the green, and drawing back a little, finishing about twenty yards short of the putting surface.

"That's a bit better, sir," said Flanagan, as he slipped the club back into the bag.

Over in the left rough, Oglesby took a hack at his ball, which scuttled low down the left edge of fairway, finishing about a hundred yards short of the flag. One by one, the rest of the members hit their second shots, all of them finding the putting surface. They gathered around Oglesby as he set up over his third.

"I say, men," Oglesby puffed, suddenly standing up straight, his face reddening. "Give a chap a little room there, won't you, I mean I can hardly breathe here."

Uncle Dickie and the rest of the members backed off a little, as Oglesby loosened his necktie and unbuttoned his shirt collar.

"Thanks awfully," he said, setting up over the ball once more. He drew his pitching wedge back slowly and deliberately, and with a mighty effort, speared it into the ground two inches behind the ball, which tumbled with the divot along the ground for about twenty yards in front of him.

"Bugger!" Oglesby shouted, stamping his foot unconvincingly.

As the group advanced up the fairway, Uncle Dickie stepped in and put an arm around Oglesby's shoulder.

"Norman," he said quietly, "if I didn't know you better, I'd say you did that on purpose."

Oglesby sniffed and straightened himself, struggling uncomfortably out of Uncle Dickie's grasp.

"Nonsense, Dickie," he snorted. "Watch this." He took another swing with the wedge, this time catching the ball well above the equator, sending it screaming past the flag and over the top of the grassy bank behind the green.

"Oops," he said. "A trifle on the thin side there perhaps," and marched off purposefully, leaving Uncle Dickie and the rest of the members in his wake. Uncle Dickie watched him curiously, stroking his chin. "Hmm," he said thoughtfully to the Maharajah, who shrugged his shoulders.

Uncle Dickie chipped up to within eight feet of the hole and stood to one side as a clump of grass appeared from behind the bank, followed by, "Bollocks!" from Oglesby, who was completely hidden from view. A few moments later, another massive clump of grass floated over the hill and landed on the back edge of the green.

"Bugger me silly!"

The dome of Oglesby's bald head popped into view as he took another hack at the ball, and this time it went rocketing high into the air off the upslope and landed softly on the back edge of the green. He puffed up the slope, made his way carefully down the other side, and marked his ball. The members were, to a man, looking on aghast at his antics.

"Who's away?" he asked.

Rabbi Hannigan, who had been twirling his long gray beard between his fingers, said, "You are, and with the fairies, if you ask me."

"Okeydokey then," Oglesby said, replacing his ball behind his marker. He went into a knock-kneed stance with his ancient hickory-shafted putter, and stabbed at the ball, which fizzed along the green, almost clipping the toes of Mickey Crutchlode, who had been attending the flag. Mickey jumped out of the way, and the ball came to rest about fifteen feet past the hole.

"All right then," said Uncle Dickie, suddenly marching into Oglesby's path as he waddled, head down, toward his ball. "Oglesby, old boy, it's about time you explained yourself."

Oglesby took a deep breath and squared up to his friends, who drew closer, listening anxiously.

"As I am largely responsible for this frightful mess, I feel that it should be me who makes the sacrifice," he said defiantly.

Not surprisingly, no one was in a hurry to disagree, but Oglesby had even more surprising news to reveal.

"Actually," he went on, "losing the old fruit and veg won't be that much of a sacrifice, as I already have all the girly kit, so to speak."

For the next few seconds, you could have heard a moth fart on the first green. Uncle Dickie was smitten by a disturbing mental image of Oglesby in a pair of fishnet stockings and a red silk teddy, and Mickey Crutchlode almost swallowed his monocle. But then, with the realization that they were all going to keep their wedding tackle, a tidal wave of relief washed over the members, and there was a barrage of backslapping, guffawing, and the like.

Only Admiral Boothely-Spifford was looking disconcertedly at Oglesby.

"Hang on here a moment," he said, brushing a lock of silver hair off his forehead, and pointing his pipe at Oglesby. "Are you saying that all these years you've been a turdburglar? You know, a shirtlifter? A chocolate starfish fighter?"

Oglesby looked horrified. "Ooh, good heavens, no, Admiral," he said. "Absolutely not. I just like the feel of ladies' clothing, that's all."

"Oh," said the Admiral. "All right, then… not a problem. In fact, so do I."

Major Norman Oglesby, now a.k.a. Norma, had just proved himself—herself?—to be exactly the sort of member that was needed at the Wood. Two weeks later, she returned from London, looking pretty damned fetching, if you asked any of the members, in a lovely tweed twin set with a string of pearls and a good stout pair of walking shoes.

When asked to say a few words, he declared in his own inimitable fashion, "I feel not as if I have taken one for the team…no, it's more like I've given two!"

Now, of course, there is a set of ladies' tees, which are cunningly placed fifty yards behind each of the championship markers, making the course 8,600 yards long. However, with Scroughtly Wood being an equal opportunity county, there is nothing to stop the lady member from playing the men's tees.

Uncle Dickie now felt content with the knowledge that all the Wood's gender, ethnic, and religious bases would be covered, what with Rabbi Hannigan, Spearman Kodogo, and Maharajah Poonsavvy being regular members of his Thursday morning ninesome. With Norma Oglesby in place, Scrought's Wood was once more set fair and ready to sail into the politically correct waters of the new millennium. Everyone in Scroughtly was happy again, with the notable exception of Oglesby Jr., who was more than a little miffed by the whole affair.

CHAPTER FOUR

The next day, the Major stood up briskly and walked over to the bay window. He looked out across the gravel courtyard at the rustic scene that lay in front of his office. Clusters of lavender wisteria hung down over the eaves of the members' quarters and its whitewashed stone and old oak beams. A crushed-pink-gravel parking lot stretched all the way to the edge of the neatly clipped putting green. The old man let his gaze wander over to the first tee where the membership was assembling for a practice round, and down the gorse-and-heather lined fairway, to the green, which nestled underneath a high, overgrown bank. There was a faraway look in the Major's sparkling blue eyes as he returned his gaze back to the courtyard and the smoke that drifted gently upward from the roof of the caddiemaster's cottage. It was a peaceful scene, in fact, a little too peaceful for the old soldier, who was looking forward with relish to the upcoming semi-centennial match between Scrought's Wood and the beastly McGregor clan from their ridiculous Tay Club, north of the border.

The Tay Club had only three holes: a par-23, a par-30, and a par-19 to finish. The McGregors' course stretched for four and a half miles along a twenty-yard-wide strip of coastline along the Firth of Tay, and the only hazards known to Uncle Dickie were the ocean on the right and three distilleries on the left. Apparently, no visitor had ever gotten past the last distillery, which of course had claimed the life of the Wood's wonderful left-hander, Sir Basil Strangely-Smallpiece, during the last match in 1949. Whilst trying to play a delicate niblick off the top of one of the vats, he slipped and fell in, drowning in single malt. A verdict of accidental death would have meant a halved match, but the Scottish coroner (a McGregor, no less) returned the preposterous verdict of suicide, simply because Sir Basil had had the decency to get out twice to go the toilet. As a boy, Uncle Dickie had caddied for Sir Basil on many occasions, learned much about the game, and was looking forward to honoring the memory of his mentor at the upcoming match.

Unfortunately, Uncle Dickie would not have the pleasure of beating the McGregors on their own sod, as the Wood was hosting. Golf's oldest trophy would be at stake, the petrified middle finger of St. Andrew, patron saint of Scotland, and the man for whom the famous "Auld Grey Toon" is named. For the previous fifty years, "The Digit," as it is known, had resided in the McGregor compound.

The clan made the long journey from their medieval encampment on the estuary of the River Tay in their one concession to modern technology, a 1958 British Leyland flatbed truck. The cab was occupied by their Chieftain, Hamish McGregor, and behind the wheel, his brother, Gregor. In the back of the ramshackle vehicle, on a variety of wooden chairs and stools, the rest of the clan, some nine men. Shuggie, Jockie, Stuart, Callum, Dirk, Dougie, and Finlay, sat huddled together as they bounced and clattered through the Northumberland countryside. A little north of the main street of Scroughtly, the truck pulled over into an easement, and the clan dismounted.

"Right, boys," shouted Hamish as the men stretched and

groaned. "Intae formation and let's show these Sassenachs how tae make an entrance."

The men were tall, short, fat, and thin, but similarly decked out in full McGregor tartan battle regalia as they marched defiantly down the main street of Scroughtly to the deafening din of "Scotland the Brave." Many of the villagers watched from the doorways and alleys as Hamish McGregor led the way with a rather skittish three-legged charcoal ewe on a leash beside him, its hooves clattering and skidding on the old cobblestones. A thin hawkish nose sprouted from his huge, unruly red beard, and beneath a tartan headband, thick bushy eyebrows hung over a pair of glinting, beady eyes.

None of the men looked sideways as they made their way past the Black Swan, over the top of the hill, past St. Mungo's parish church, and on down the street to the Pig & Spigot, where most of the menfolk of Scroughtly had gathered to watch them pass. As the clan approached the pub, the music started to wane and then died completely.

Hamish stopped abruptly, causing the group of men behind him to stumble into one another. He spun around and glared, his dark eyes flashing angrily from one man to another. The men shifted nervously, avoiding his stare, and sidled around until they had separated themselves from a fat clansman in the center of the group, who was fumbling nervously with the knobs on a large yellow and gray boom box.

"Shuggie, you bastard," Hamish hissed murderously under his breath, glancing sideways at the crowd. "Ah gave you money for batteries, did ah not?"

The previous evening, Hugh McGregor, known to the boys as "Shuggie," had looked at the eight dead size-D batteries, and decided that he could replace four of them, and the machine would probably work just as well. He had spent the rest of the money on three more pints of Tartan Bitter. The night before, when this notion had been camouflaged behind all the other brilliant ideas in Shuggie's mind—and seventeen previous pints of Tartan Bitter—it had seemed perfectly logical. But now, he and his flash of genius stood alone in the middle of the street staring at Hamish, who was trembling as if he was about to erupt. Shuggie swallowed hard and straightened himself up.

"Er, aah, ah suppose Jockie could play," he stammered.

The rest of the men stared at Shuggie in disbelief, as Hamish drew himself up to his full height and stared at the sky for a moment.

"Aye, Shuggie," he said quietly. "But Jockie plays the bagpipes like Stuart does the sword dance, doesn't he?" Hamish looked over at the small crowd of villagers outside the pub, who were silent and obviously trying to hear what was being said. He smiled nastily and gave a cheery little wave. "Hello, everybody, how are you?" Then he turned to Shuggie, who was also smiling and waving. Hamish exploded.

"WHICH IS WHY STUART HAS ONLY ONE TOE ON HIS LEFT FOOT, YOU DOZY BOLLOCKS!" he screamed. He spun around and pointed a long, bony finger into the group of men. "JOCKIE, GET YER PIPES OOT, AN PLAY!"

An elderly clansman at the back of the group rummaged

through a battered duffel bag and shouldered an old set of pipes, which he began to inflate with a tuneless skirl.

Hamish winced and, with an angry nod to the crowd outside the pub, he motioned to his gaggle of kilted followers and jerked on the leash.

"C'mon, Brenna," he grunted, and the clan set off once more, down the hill and out of the village, into the narrow hedge-lined road known as Hadrian's Lane, which led to the Wood. Some moments later, they turned into the driveway of the Scrought's Wood Golf Club. The evil wailing of Jockie's pipes had preceded them, and on the veranda, Uncle Dickie and the members were waiting.

The fiendish din of the bagpipes finally died and Hamish stepped forward. "Gussett," he snapped curtly, barely nodding his head toward Uncle Dickie.

"Good day to you, McGregor," Uncle Dickie replied, extending his hand and examining the giant bush of tangled red hair that sprouted from Hamish's face.

"I see you're still trying to swallow that cat!"

"Aye, whatever," Hamish shot back, ignoring the out-stretched hand, "Yer a very funny man. Let's skip the pleasant-ries, Gussett. Mah daddy hated yer daddy and ah hate you, ya toffee-nosed old fart." He motioned toward the group of kilted men behind him.

"So, where are we bunkin' up?"

"You can sleep in the hedge behind the first tee, for all I care, though we have prepared the Dormy House, as is customary," Uncle Dickie said. "We would appreciate it, however, should you or any of your clansmen intend to light a fire, if you would use the fireplace this time. Also, your goat must stay outside."

"Ho, ho bloody ho, Gussett," McGregor said. "You're absolutely hilarious. This sheep sleeps where we sleep."

"In that case," replied Uncle Dickie, looking down his nose at the quivering animal, "I imagine it must sleep very lightly."

"Aye," McGregor said. "Anyway, we'll be roasting a wee haggis tonight, if you or any of yer members have big enough bollocks tae join us."

Uncle Dickie rubbed his chin thoughtfully. "Let me see," he said. "Pickled genitalia, minced eyelids, and shredded nostrils all wrapped up in a sheep's bladder and boiled for hours. Sounds yummy, but taking into consideration that most of us here have already had dysentery at least once, I think we'll pass."

"Please yerselves," said McGregor, "ye dinnae ken what yer missin', though."

"We'll see you on the tee at eight o'clock sharp tomorrow morning," said Uncle Dickie. "And, by the way, old boy, we have a dress code here at Scrought's Wood, so if I were you, I wouldn't wear that skirt."

Oglesby, who was wearing an enormous pair of tweed culottes and a silk blouse, harrumphed loudly on the veranda behind Uncle Dickie.

"Oh, yes," said Uncle Dickie, smiling apologetically at Oglesby. "Yes, well, whatever. Wear what you want, McGregor."

Hamish scowled at Uncle Dickie and said, "For yer information, Gussett, we will all be wearing the McGregor battle kilt with full ratskin sporrans and toories and there's bugger all you can do about it!"

"I see," Uncle Dickie said with a strange smile. "So, I imagine, like a true Scotsman, you'll wear nothing under your kilt?"

"No!" shouted McGregor gleefully. "It's all in perfect workin' order." The other clan members threw back their heads and roared with laughter.

"As you wish, McGregor," Uncle Dickie said. "We shall see you in the morning." He turned quietly, and with a sly smile, led the members inside.

The next morning, dawn cracked hard with a distant flash and the ominous rumble of a thunderstorm. Uncle Dickie sat with the rest of the members in the dining room and was about to tuck into a plate of ham and eggs when the door burst open, and in marched Hamish McGregor. He swaggered over to where Uncle Dickie sat, leaned over the table, and picked up a fried egg from his plate. The room went silent as he tilted back his head and dropped the egg into the hole in his bushy red beard. The yoke dribbled out the side of his mouth as he chewed noisily and lowered his face to within inches of Uncle Dickie's.

"Ah'm goin' tae eat yer breakfast, and yer lunch as well, ya dozy old bastard." Uncle Dickie reached down into his lap and produced a crisp, linen napkin. He reached up and dabbed the side of Hamish's mouth.

"You'd better wear a bib then," Uncle Dickie said calmly, nodding down toward Hamish's sporran. "I know that's the only skirt you own."

"Oh, very good, old boy," Hamish mimicked. "But you'll be smilin' on the other side of yer fizzog after I've dealt with ye this morning! There's only one thing that ah need tae do first. Ah feel a pressing urge tae mark mah territory, so tae speak. So where's yer dumper?"

Uncle Dickie motioned behind him to the locker room door. "Help yourself," he said, smiling pleasantly. "And give my regards to the better part of you, when you flush."

Hamish grunted, spun around, and made his way hurriedly to the locker room. When he had gone, the buzz of conversation started once again in the dining room. Maharajah Poonsavvy sat opposite Uncle Dickie, his dark skin in stark contrast to a magnificent yellow silk costume. A giant ruby and gold brooch glowed from the center of his turban.

"What an extremely unpleasant fellow, Dickie," he said in his singsong Punjabi lilt. I am, as you know, a pacifist at heart, but I find myself at this moment fighting an overwhelming urge to go into the toilet and wipe the floor with that hideous beard."

Uncle Dickie smiled over at his old friend. "Don't worry, Poony, we'll be wiping the floor with them soon enough." He took a sip from his teacup, wiped his mouth, and winked mischievously. "I'll see you on the first tee," he said, getting up and making his way over to the locker room door. Once inside, he pushed open the swinging doors to the toilets, and started to wash his hands at one of the basins. Behind, he heard McGregor straining and grunting in one of the stalls.

"Ah, Hamish, that's the smell of fear, if I'm not mistaken," he said. Behind him, the grunting stopped.

"Up yours, Gussett," Hamish replied. "You're a beaten man, an' ye know it."

Uncle Dickie dried his hands with a small towel, tossed it into a wicker basket, and walked over to the door of the stall. He gave it a swift, hard kick, and it banged open, revealing Hamish seated on the pot, with his kilt hiked up around his belly.

"Oooh, I see," said Uncle Dickie. "You really don't wear anything under that thing."

Hamish glared back, undaunted. "Ah'll be right with ye, Gussett," he grunted, staring at Uncle Dickie as he gave another mighty heave. Uncle Dickie gave a frown of distaste and turned on his heel. As he walked toward the exit, he heard a heavy splash.

"Remember, Hamish," he called as he opened the door, "when your head starts to cave in, you should stop squeezing."

Meanwhile, Dwilby the terrier had found something very curious behind the Dormy House. A shaggy little crossbreed, Dwilby was owned by Agnes, the wife of caddiemaster Seamus Flanagan. Like most terriers, he considered himself to be the top dog. He had caught a whiff of something different, and was sniffing around, when he came across a strange woolly animal, tethered to a drainpipe. Dwilby had no idea what this creature was, but it smelled okay, and he had made up his mind that he was going to give it a damned good seeing-to. It took him a while to get a decent grip, as Brenna played hard to get, kicking, and backing up against the wall, but finally, he was able to get his teeth into the wool on her back, and begin a very serious relationship.

The air was thick and humid as the first of the nine matches got under way. Maharajah Poonsavvy watched as Gregor McGregor swished away his tee shot, the pleats of his kilt lilting on the follow-through. Uncle Dickie, who was to play Hamish McGregor in the final match, stood close by the Maharajah and whispered, "Poonsavvy, old boy, leggings on at the fourth. Okay?" The turban-clad Maharajah gave a wink and set off down the fairway, followed by Pogo, his one-legged caddie, who slung the clubs easily over his shoulder and hopped down the slope of the first tee, wearing his strange boot with its tennis-racket-sized sole. The historic match got under way, to a strange mix of bleating and growling from behind the Dormy House.

The McGregor clansmen were considerably younger and fitter than the members, and seemed to be obvious favorites. It was 11:10 A.M. when Uncle Dickie squared off against the McGregor chieftain, who wore an evil smile as he swaggered onto the first tee. "Ahm goin' tae beat you like a big bass drum, Gussett, and ahm goin' tae enjoy every minute of it."

"Yes, and the next Pope will no doubt be a Presbyterian," replied Uncle Dickie resolutely. "Hit it and stop slobbering."

McGregor threw down his ball and, without a tee or a practice swing, drew the club back in a slow, deliberate windup and hit a vicious, hard fade down the left half, finishing about 280 yards away, in the center of the fairway.

Flanagan, Uncle Dickie's caddie, looked aghast as McGregor's tee shot came to rest. He stepped forward, and offered the two bags of clubs to his boss.

Uncle Dickie raised an eyebrow and smiled once more. "That's a great shot with that method, McGregor," he said. "Now, watch this."

He chose one of his eleven drivers, teed his ball up high, and with a gentle waft, hit an elegant little draw about 175 yards down the left-hand side. McGregor looked at him and said, "Mah God, Gussett. Is that all yiv got? This is goin' tae be like clubbin' seals."

As they walked down the first fairway, a plaintive wail was heard, far off in the distance. Hamish stopped, cocked his ear, and looked quizzically at Uncle Dickie. "What the bloody hell was tha'?" he said.

As Uncle Dickie reached his ball, another pitiful shriek floated on the wind. "Music to my ears," he replied, as he addressed his second shot, and gave an exaggerated waggle.

McGregor, who was marching quickly toward his ball, stopped, and whirled around to face the old man. "Hey, Gussett," he shouted, in the middle of Uncle Dickie's setup. "You look lonely back there. Would ye like tae join me?"

Unfazed, Uncle Dickie sent off a low, raking draw that almost took the tassel off McGregor's toorie, and rolled to a stop twelve feet from the cup.

"I'll be with you in a moment, McGregor," he yelled, as another scream of agony was heard in the distance.

The first hole was halved in four, but things took a wrong turn for Uncle Dickie as he lost the second and third to pars from McGregor, who was gloating horribly as they reached the next tee.

The fourth at Scrought's Wood is a picturesque par-3 that borders the gardens of Gussett Hall on the right and an abandoned slate quarry on the left.

From tee to green on the left side, there is a three-hundred-foot vertical drop to the floor of the pit, and on the right are Auntie Myrtle's vegetables (of which Uncle Dickie is her favorite, she says), protected by a stone wall, some twenty feet high.

The only way to get from tee to green is through a patch of shoulder-high hawthorn, gorse, and brambles known as Beelzebub's Beard. But from the tee, there was no obvious way through.

McGregor chose a 4-iron and hit a high draw, some twenty feet from the hole. "Follow that, Gussett," he roared.

Uncle Dickie found the front edge with one of his drivers, and then bent over, picking up his tee, saying, "Follow me, McGregor," with an evil smirk.

He then rummaged in one of his golf bags, pulling out two pairs of heavy waxed overtrousers, one of which he gave to Flanagan. The two men pulled them on, and there was a lightness in Uncle Dickie's step as he set off after McGregor, who was by this time standing at the edge of the Beard, scratching his head, and looking puzzled.

"How the bloody hell dae we get tae the green?" he asked incredulously.

"I have no idea how you're getting there, but I shall be walking through here," said Uncle Dickie, as he marched purposefully into the thick, thorny scrub. Flanagan perched both bags on his shoulders and struggled through in Uncle Dickie's wake.

McGregor stood looking confused and angry, and yelled after them, "Ah canny get through here, Gussett. It'll slash me intae wee pieces!"

"Sounds like a personal problem to me, McGregor, old boy," Uncle Dickie called back. "Around here we dress accordingly, for in the game of golf, one must take on Mother Nature, both her elements and her terrain."

"Oof," cried Flanagan, as a hawthorn branch recoiled, catching him smartly across the ear.

McGregor paced furiously back and forth between the wall and the edge of the quarry, searching for a way through but, clearly, there was nowhere to go, except straight ahead.

Flanagan and Uncle Dickie stood on the other side of the Beard, looking back at the forlorn and angry figure, some seventy yards behind them.

"Hamish!" cried Uncle Dickie, who was grinning broadly, and looking at his wristwatch. "If you don't hurry up, I'll have to eat my own lunch!"

"Damn ye tae hell, Gussett!" Hamish roared, as suddenly he charged into the vicious tangle in front of him. He got about five yards into the undergrowth before stopping stone dead and letting out a strangulated, high-pitched wail. It was then he realized where all the screaming and moaning had been coming from.

"Aargh!" he shrieked. "Ooh, mah poor wee danglies! Oooh, Lord have mercy!"

It was a horrible few moments to listen to as McGregor

struggled through the wiry scrub. Every time he lifted his arms to protect his face from the thin whip-like branches, the lower thorns would tear at his legs and groin. All the time, though, he kept his gaze locked on Uncle Dickie. Eventually it was over, and he stood, ashen-faced, on the other side of Beelzebub's Beard.

"Yer an evil old man, Gussett," he gasped. His legs were torn and bleeding.

"I tried to warn you, McGregor," said Uncle Dickie. "But I recall you telling me you would dress however you desired. So, let's play, shall we?"

McGregor limped to the green's edge and it was clear that the coarse wool of his kilt was aggravating whatever ghastly wounds lay beneath. He was two up and managed a half at the fourth. But, effectively, the match was over.

Every full swing caused his kilt to swish back and forth, and the McGregor chieftain, like all of his clansmen who had played the fourth before him, was soon squealing and flinching on every shot.

Uncle Dickie won every hole from there on and the match was over on the thirteenth green.

Back at the clubhouse, the full extent of the damage was evident. Scrought's Wood had won the match 8½ to ½ only because, despite being warned, Major Norma Oglesby had chosen to wear a tweed skirt that morning, apparently defending his decision by saying, "Trousers make my bottom look big."

The McGregors tended to their wounds in the Dormy House and then assembled underneath the back veranda where the members waited for the presentation of the finger. Uncle Dickie, large brandy in hand, walked down the steps to meet them. Hamish stood defiantly at the front, holding Brenna on a short leash.

"Before you go, McGregor, I have something for you," he said. He snapped his fingers and Crump, the wine steward, appeared, holding a cloth bag. Uncle Dickie reached into it and pulled out a pair of tartan underpants. "I believe this is the McGregor tartan," he said, putting them back into the bag and handing it to McGregor.

McGregor tossed the bag over his shoulder, where it was caught by Shuggie, who stuffed it painfully behind his back. "Never!" Hamish shouted. "Not in my lifetime."

He turned around and barked, "Callum, give Gussett the finger."

A huge, bearded clansman walked gingerly forward and, with a grimace, gave Uncle Dickie an ancient-looking wooden box and limped back into the huddle of men.

"Thank you, sir," said Uncle Dickie. "We shall take good care of it."

"See tha' ye do," said McGregor. "For in fifty years our kinfolk will be claimin' it back." Once again locking eyes with Uncle Dickie, he raised his bandaged arm in the air and motioned backward, just as Dwilby trotted out of the bushes to his left and headed for the back door to the kitchens. Brenna spotted the little dog immediately and started to strain the leash toward him, her three hooves scratching at the gravel. Hamish looked over at the dog and then at Brenna, an expression of horror on his face.

"You didn't," he hissed. Brenna looked up at him, and then bleated at Dwilby, who had stopped to watch.

Hamish looked at the sky, and screamed, "ABOUT FACE!"

And, with that, Jockie McGregor shouldered his pipes, and raising a deafening skirl, the clan turned around clumsily and hobbled down the driveway, leaving Hamish at the rear.

"STOP, YA BASTARDS!" he roared, and once again the men stumbled into one another, as Hamish pushed and shoved his way to the front, dragging Brenna behind him. He straightened his toorie, and pulled his torn kilt into shape. "Right," he said. "Let's go home, boys."

Jockie the tuneless piper cranked it up again, and off they limped between the high hedges of the driveway. Once they were around the corner and out of sight, the din stopped for about thirty seconds and then started again.

Uncle Dickie dipped into his waistcoat pocket, pulled out a small tin, and twisted some wax onto the tips of his luxurious mustache.

He winked at the Maharajah and said, "I do hope they fit."

CHAPTER FIVE

The din of the bagpipes faded as the McGregors marched away between the high honeysuckle hedges that lined Hadrian's Lane, the little road that led to the Wood from town. Uncle Dickie turned around to face the members gathered on the veranda and broke into a broad grin. He clapped his hands together and rubbed them vigorously. "Righty-ho," he exclaimed. "Gentlemen, I believe it's time for an evening of self-indulgence, if ever there was one!" He motioned to Crump, the wine steward, who stood in the doorway. "Crump, crack open a case of the fifty-year-old reserve malt, and two cases of '56 Margaux, and set us up in the card room, if you please."

Uncle Dickie seemed visibly younger as he strode into the old clubhouse, humming loudly as he went. "You know," he shouted to no one in particular, "it's been a while since we had any music in this old place." He turned to Brigadier Kodogo. "Spearman, old boy, why don't you go and find old Willoughby Hurd, and see if he can't rustle us up some live entertainment, what, what?"

"Of course, Dickie," Kodogo said, his perfect white teeth bursting into view on an enormous, coal-black face. He hurried off down the hallway toward the secretary-manager's office. He tapped on the door, opened it and walked in to find Willoughby behind his desk, his nose buried in, *Ferret Fancier* magazine.

Willoughby was something of a mystery at the club, having just appeared one day, and taken up residence in the secretary-manager's office, which had been vacant for some years. By the time Willoughby had been discovered, it was apparent that an inmate of the psychiatric wing of nearby St. Egbert's infirmary had gone missing, but the strange, myopic old man had done such a good job of cleaning and refiling everything in the office that Uncle Dickie had hired him on the spot. An anal retentive, obsessive-compulsive former librarian, Willoughby was, as Uncle Dickie said, "Mad as a sack of ex-wives, but easier to deal with."

"Briggsy, old dear," Willoughby said, quickly dropping the magazine onto the desk. "What can I do for you?"

"Willoughby, Uncle Dickie wants you to find somebody to play some music here tonight, you know, like a live band perhaps?"

Willoughby took off his impossibly thick glasses and rubbed his eyes. He brought his forearm up to the end of his nose, and looked at his watch.

"But it's six-thirty P.M. already," he said, "How the hell am I supposed to find anyone now?"

"I don't know," Kodogo said, "but the old boy is in a great mood, so do your best, okay?" He grinned broadly and thumped the desk. "That's the spirit!"

Willoughby stared in horror for a moment at the greasy spot the Brigadier had left on his desk, took out a linen hanky, and rubbed it away. He tossed the hanky neatly into the wastepaper basket, sighed, and reached under his desk for the phone book. "Very well," he said, "but don't expect the London Philharmonic."

A steady hum of conversation, interrupted by an occasional

roar of laughter, could be heard down the musty old hallway. Portraits of members long since passed away hung on the walls along with their ancient golf clubs and dusty trophies. In the trophy case, back in its rightful place, sat the old box that contained the digit. Uncle Dickie paused in front of a particularly impressive oil painting of a very distinguished-looking old gentleman leaning on a left-handed niblick. He was dressed in a World War I flying suit, with a leather helmet and goggles pushed up over his forehead, a silk cravat around his throat, and a mischievous twinkle in his dark brown eyes.

Uncle Dickie stood rigidly to attention, saluted the painting, and said, as his eyes moistened, "Sir Basil, this one was for you, old boy."

Uncle Dickie strode down the corridor to the card room door, and shouted over the din, "A toast, gentlemen and lady," as he gestured toward Major Norma Oglesby. The room fell silent, and everyone got to their feet.

"To Sir Basil Strangely-Smallpiece. May his memory live forever."

"Sir Basil," repeated the men solemnly, as they raised their glasses. Uncle Dickie slung his arm around the enormous shoulders of Reggie Carstairs, as they both tossed back their brandies in one swallow. "Reggie, old boy," Uncle Dickie said, "Did I ever tell you that Sir Basil was awarded the Victoria Cross for valor in the Great War? You know, he single-handedly cut the German lines of communication in Belgium."

"No, Dickie," Carstairs boomed. "How the devil did he do that?"

"Well," said Uncle Dickie, "He ate their carrier pigeon. Tough as an old boot, by all accounts. Actually, he said it was the only bad meal he ever had in Belgium. Had to drink an entire bottle of 1876 Vintage Port to get rid of the taste. Look," Uncle Dickie pointed, "there's Kodogo over there with Poonsavvy and Mickey Crutchlode, why don't we join them?"

Uncle Dickie sat down in a large overstuffed leather chair, and slapped Kodogo on the back. "Well, old boy, that was a day's fun, was it not?" he said.

Kodogo's face was shining as he wiped the Guinness suds from his enormous handlebar mustache with a linen handkerchief.

"Damned right, it was," he roared. "I was just reminiscing with the boys here about that time in India when you and I were fighting the fuzzy-wuzzy, you know?"

"Careful, Briggsy," chortled the Maharajah. "I am one of those fuzzy people, you know!"

Kodogo looked confused.

"Oh, yes," he said. "So you are." He stared vacantly into space for a moment. "Now that I come to think of it, so am I...."

"Anyway, though," he continued, "there we were, hacking our way through the jungle with machetes, swatting mosquitoes the size of canaries, with the camp bearers following behind. All of a sudden we broke through into a clearing, so we decided to set up camp for the evening." Brigadier Kodogo lowered his voice, and leaned in toward the center of the table, his cheeks glistening.

"Then, as the bearers began to erect the first tent, out of

nowhere, a huge tiger came crashing from the undergrowth right into Uncle Dickie's face, like this."

Kodogo suddenly stood up from his chair, raised his hands in the air, drew back his lips in a fearsome snarl, and, at the top of his voice, yelled "ROOOARRR!"

Then he put both hands on the edge of the table, bent over, and said quietly to Poonsavvy, "I soiled myself."

"Yes," said the Maharajah, "I am imagining that you most probably had a legitimate reason to do so."

"No, Poony, not then," replied Kodogo, looking a little startled. "I mean just now, when I stood up and roared."

He staggered off toward the locker room door, as the room, which had been silenced by his loud outburst, broke up into gales of hysterical laughter.

"I have a spare pair of bloomers, old trout," yelled Major Norma Oglesby as she held open the door to the toilet.

"Up yours, you old tart," Kodogo yelled back as the door slammed behind him.

At the corner of the bar, Uncle Dickie sat down, and put his arm around his old friend Bertie Featherstone, who, stuffed and mounted, had silently been presiding over all the goings-on in the room. Nine old duffers sat at two tables, telling exaggerated tales and outright lies, laughing and drinking, drinking and laughing.

Every one of them had been a hero, and a loyal friend to Uncle Dickie. Each had a story to tell and had made a journey through life that would end at this golf club, for they were each other's only real family. For a moment, Uncle Dickie let his eyes glaze over, and his mind wander back to the battlefields, and the dark, underground war rooms where these friendships had first been forged. The match with the McGregors had stirred old feelings within him, and he wondered if it were possible that the events of this day might mark the last time he would ever see active service, or feel the heat of battle. He hoped not.

Suddenly, the room was silenced by a huge crash, as an elderly man in a hospital gown fell over the small drum kit he was carrying through the doorway. Uncle Dickie was startled out of his daydream, as two others followed, one with a trumpet, and another with an accordion. Willoughby Hurd rushed in and helped the fallen man to his feet. Fortunately, both the drummer and the trumpet player were wearing underwear, but to the dismay of all present, the crack of the accordion player's backside yawned into full view through the back of his gown as he bent over to put down his instrument.

Willoughby Hurd sheepishly approached Uncle Dickie, who was looking on, slack jawed, as the trio set up in the corner.

"Hurd, you idiot," he said, "Who the hell are they?"

Willoughby wrung his hands anxiously and genuflected a couple of times. "I'm sorry, Major General Gussett, but it's the best I could do at such short notice," he stammered. "They're from the psychiatric wing of St. Egbert's Infirmary, my old stomping grounds and where my sister works, and she assures me that they are really quite good. It had to be either them or the Legendary Yeovil Formation Yodeling Team."

"Wait a minute," said Uncle Dickie, "Your sister? Isn't she deaf?"

"Well, no sir…er, not entirely," Willoughby waffled, looking into space. "Well, sort of, legally speaking, she might be." He looked at Uncle Dickie and sighed, straightening up.

"Yes, she is, sir, deaf as a post, actually."

Suddenly the drummer stood up from behind his kit and announced at the top of his voice, "Ladies and gentlemen, will you please welcome, here for one night only at the lovely Scrought's Wood Golf Club, Mister Perry Stalsis, and the Colon Muscle Band!"

Everyone in the room looked more than a little dumbfounded, as the trio launched into an energetic but tuneless polka. Willoughby Hurd walked quietly backward, slipped a handkerchief out of his pocket, and used it to grasp the handle of the side door to the veranda. He sidled out, as Uncle Dickie turned to the Maharajah and yelled over the din, "Good Lord, Poony, I haven't heard anything quite that obnoxious since Penfold's cat got trapped in the ball washer!"

Reggie Carstairs held his head in his hands. "Please, God, make it stop," he said.

The door to the locker room toilet opened slowly, and Kodogo reappeared, directly behind the band. He stopped, apparently transfixed by the sight of the accordion player's buttocks, which were jiggling up and down to that crazy polka beat. He turned around very slowly, and slipped back into the toilet.

Finally the song ended, and Kodogo peered back out from behind the door. He marched quickly around the band and stopped in front of the accordion player, as the members looked on.

"Sir," he said at the top of his voice," unless I am very much mistaken, we still have a dress code at this club. Do you know you're not wearing any underwear?"

"I do, sir," replied the man, "but it always makes the drummer cry, so we stopped playing it."

There was a collective groan at the old joke, but Kodogo was not to be denied.

"Well, listen," he said, wagging his finger sternly. "I've shat myself once already tonight, and if I hear any more of whatever the hell that was, I'm just liable to do it again, and while that would be a personal best, I think the rest of the chaps could do without it. Do you know any Frank Sinatra?"

"I know the man personally, sir; in fact I slept with him last night."

"Good," said Kodogo, "then play some of him."

The sounds of a discordant "New York, New York," floated down on the breeze to the caddie shed, and beyond to the caddiemaster's cottage. Inside, Seamus Flanagan had just gotten out of the bathtub and was drying himself in the tiny bathroom. Dwilby, the mongrel terrier, was scratching furiously at the back door.

"Agnes," Flanagan yelled. "Let that bloody dog out, will ye?"

"Let him in, ye mean," Agnes muttered to herself, as she walked across the kitchen and pulled open the back door. Dwilby shot in and trotted quickly through the house to the bedroom where Flanagan now stood with his back to the dog, on the other side of the bed.

Flanagan was the only caddie at Scrought's Wood with no military background. He had always been just a caddie, and Uncle Dickie had taken a shine to him during one round at Portmarnock in which he had played particularly well. From that day, no one else had ever caddied for the old man, and Flanagan and his wife had lived in the caddiemaster's cottage at the club.

As Flanagan bent over to put on his underwear, Dwilby hopped silently onto the bed and, just as his master lifted his left foot off the floor to search for the leghole in his Y-fronts, the little dog jammed his cold, wet nose deep between the cheeks of Flanagan's backside, and took a good sniff.

"AAAAARGH!" Flanagan screamed as he jerked bolt upright, banging his head on the windowsill and getting tangled up in his shorts. Holding his head with one hand and the shorts in the other, he took two hops sideways and fell into the wardrobe.

Dwilby sneezed violently, and started to scratch at the bedclothes until he had rucked them into a comfortable heap. Then he turned around twice, lay down, and began to energetically lick his balls.

Agnes Flanagan, hearing the commotion, put her head around the doorway.

"Did the dog get ye in the arse again, Seamus? A'hve telt ye ta be more careful a million times, ye know that wee dog is trained to catch rats. He loves t'get into tight places."

She clapped her hand to her mouth, stifling a laugh, as her

husband struggled out of the open wardrobe. Flanagan painfully dragged himself to his feet and glared at his wife.

"That's very helpful, Agnes, but do ah look like ah've got rats up mah arse?"

Agnes was shaking uncontrollably, and laughing fit to burst. "No," she managed, "but sometimes y'smell like y' do! Maybe Dwilby saw one peekin' oot!"

She shrieked with laughter and fell onto the bed, where Dwilby set about licking the tears of mirth from her face.

"That's it!" Seamus spat, pointing a finger at the dog. "His bollocks are comin' off tomorrow an' no argument. Things have come to a pretty pass in this house, when a man can't even put his jockeys on for fear of bein' probed by a canine pervert."

Agnes grabbed the little dog and held him tight, her face suddenly dark. "Well, that's okay," she said. "Just as long as y'don't mind losin' yer own in the middle of the night. You just keep yer arse t'the wall and you'll be fine."

Flanagan pulled on his trousers and a flannel shirt, and examined himself in the mirror. He rubbed the back of his head. "Ah don't know, Agnes," he grumbled. "Ah don't know which is colder," he gestured toward the dog. "His nose or your heart. Ah'm off t'the Pig & Spigot fer a few pints with the boys."

Agnes scooped Dwilby off the bed and brushed past him. "Aye, well, just keep that car between the hedges on the way home, y'old goat, an' lay off the pickled eggs. Just one of those paint-stripping farts in our room an ah'll have the dog on ye again!" She roared with laughter.

Flanagan gingerly pulled on a cloth cap over the reddening bump on his bald spot and strode past his wife and out of the bedroom.

"Away an' boil yer head," he muttered under his breath, slamming the back door behind him.

The gravel scrunched beneath his boots as he marched the few yards over to the caddie shed, where the back door lay open. Inside, the caddies, Tweezer, Herpy, Pogo, and Thirsty were playing cards and watching a soccer match on the old black-and-white television, while Mills, Boon, and Stanley Beamish played pitch-and-toss in the corner. Flanagan poked his head through the crack in the door.

"Right, lads, it's time fer a skinful!"

"Aye, about time too," said Thirsty, looking at his wristwatch. "I'm in severe danger of soberin' up."

"Oh, dearie me, we can't have that," said Flanagan. "Tweezer! Are you ridin' or rollin' tonight?"

"I wouldn't trust you to drive a nail into a bar of soap, Flanagan," said Tweezer. "I'll be in my chariot as usual." He pulled himself off the wooden chair he had been on, and into the specially designed wheelchair with its fat tires, and a strange-looking harness for carrying a golf bag behind.

"Suit yerself, it's uphill all the way. C'mon, lads, into the caddie wagon!"

Outside, Flanagan slid open the door to his old Volkswagen minivan, and the caddies piled in. He cranked the clapped-out engine and with a whining of belts and pulleys it coughed into life. Flanagan let out a whoop, gunned it, and spun around on the gravel, showering Tweezer and his wheelchair with the tiny stones. Tweezer dusted himself down and started to pump the wheels of the chair with his massive upper arms.

"Arseholes," he muttered as he rolled off down the driveway. "I'm surrounded by arseholes."

Back in the card room, the party was in full swing. Perry Stalsis and the boys had hit their stride, and Major Norma Oglesby, resplendent in a sequined muumuu the size of a small gazebo, had the microphone and was belting out a surprisingly tuneful rendition of "I've got a lovely bunch of coconuts."

Reggie Carstairs was face down in a mountainous plate of bangers and mash, sweating profusely. He seized the moment and heckled, "Nonsense, Oglesby old girl," as a pea shot from his mouth, landing in Maharajah Poonsavvy's turban. "Surely you mean, I *had* a lovely bunch of coconuts!"

Whoops and cheers resounded around the room, as the Maharajah searched for the offending vegetable in his head-piece.

"Really, Carstairs, old chap, I would appreciate it greatly if you could limit the expulsion of food from your body to those orifices specifically designed for such purposes."

Uncle Dickie, who had for a moment been lost in his private thoughts, slapped his thighs and guffawed loudly, raising his glass in the air. "The troops are in fine fettle tonight!" he roared.

"Yes," Kodogo replied, "but I suspect they'll feel a little the worse for wear in the morning."

Uncle Dickie hammered the bar. "Nonsense," he said, his blue eyes twinkling. "The man that worries about tomorrow forgets to enjoy today. Live in the present old boy, for the present is all we ever have!" He thumped the bar once more.

The door to the card room opened slowly, and to everyone's surprise, Aunt Myrtle walked in, holding a dusty old bottle. She and Agnes Flanagan were the only two females who ever visited the clubhouse, albeit infrequently, so her arrival caused quite a stir. Norma Oglesby straightened her muumuu uncomfortably, as Auntie Myrtle broke into a wide smile, and placed the bottle on the table in front of her.

"At ease, men," she said laughingly. "I just heard there was cause for celebration, that's all, so I brought you a bottle of my famous gut-primer."

"Darling," said Uncle Dickie. "How very thoughtful of you. I'm sure the boys will feel all the better for it, come the dawn! Crump, give the boys a shot of gut-primer if you please."

Crump took the bottle, and disappeared into the back bar for a moment and returned with a small tray of shot glasses filled with a cloudy, brownish fluid. He had an almost imperceptible hint of a grin on his face as he handed it across the bar.

"There you are, sir," he smiled. "These'll put lead in your pencil!"

Uncle Dickie took the tray, and offered one of the glasses to Kodogo, who viewed it with suspicion. Knowing that argument would be futile, the Brigadier smiled weakly and asked, "Dear God, Dickie, do I have to?"

"Lines your stomach," said Uncle Dickie." Get it down your

neck, and don't be such a fairy. You'll thank me in the morning."

Kodogo held his enormous nose, knocked the contents of the glass back in one, and found himself barely able to keep it down. Uncle Dickie slapped him on the back a couple of times as he dry-heaved, and then caught his breath, gasping, "My God, what the hell is in that stuff?"

"I'm led to believe that raw goat's liver and a duck egg are the main ingredients," said Uncle Dickie, turning to Auntie Myrtle.

"And a secret ingredient," Myrtle said.

"Working on the theory that a goat can keep anything down, and a duck never appears to be hung over," Uncle Dickie chortled. "Look at Rabbi Hannigan. He has a shot of it morning and night, and he's fit as a fiddle at seventy-eight!"

Kodogo looked over at the old clergyman who was in the corner, dancing by himself, hopping up and down, his hands twirling high above his head.

"Mad as a pit bull, of course," said Uncle Dickie. "Convinced St. Patrick was Moses' second cousin. That's his kosher Irish dancing. He gets into it when he's has a few pops on board, but you have to admit, he's in great shape."

One by one, the members tossed back the shots, gagged, and reached for their drinks to kill the taste. Aunt Myrtle kissed Uncle Dickie on the cheek, and blew a kiss to the rest of the boys. "Have fun," she said mischievously. Then she turned and walked gracefully out of the card room, around the corner, and down the hallway toward the trophy cases and the front door.

The little yellow van trundled slowly up the hill toward the village of Scroughtly where, in the dimly lit main street, the cheers and refrains of another celebration mingled with the peat smoke that drifted across the thatched rooftops. The din came from the Pig & Spigot, one of the village's two pubs, where almost the entire population of Scroughtly, about 150 souls, had turned out to toast the victory over the McGregors.

Uncle Dickie owned the golf course and all the surrounding land. He allowed his workers to grow their own crops and graze their own cattle, and the only thing he asked in return was that they guard the privacy of his precious club, which they did with a passion. Uncle Dickie loved the people of Scroughtly, especially the children, many of whose education he had provided throughout the years, and he thought of the club, the town, and the surrounding area, as his kingdom. The villagers were happy that, at least around these parts, Uncle Dickie was king.

Flanagan parked the van a little way down the street from the Pig & Spigot, and as they tumbled out, the caddies heard the pub door open and a toast to "Uncle Dickie," followed by a loud cheer and much laughter. "Aye," said Flanagan, pulling on his cap as he marched toward the door. "Sounds like they started without us. Come on, lads."

"Give us a hand, you bastards," shouted Pogo, who had eased himself out of the van and was hopping precariously toward the pub, holding his prosthetic limb under his arm. He had contracted gangrene after being wounded in the Burmese jungle, and his right leg had been crudely amputated in a Japanese prisoner of war camp. After the war, Uncle Dickie had put him to work at the club, and over the years, he had many artificial limbs made for Pogo. But the old soldier simply had an aversion to them, and had chosen to devise for himself a giant-soled shoe, which made it easier for him to balance on one leg, as he hopped around the golf course with a bag on his back. He really only used the leg when he was standing still for long periods of time, such as the drinking session he was about to take part in at the Pig & Spigot. These days, though, he was tired in the evenings and occasionally he swallowed his pride and asked for help.

Thirsty walked back, put his arm around the old man, and levered him, hip-to-hip, toward the door. "I can't understand it, Pogo," he laughed. "But your missing leg gives me a bad back."

Flanagan burst through the door and into the pub. He flung off his hat as he went and yelled at the top of his voice, "All right, boys and girls, the drinks are on Uncle Dickie!" The crowd cheered as Flanagan pulled a wad of notes from his pocket and waved them high in the air as he and the caddies pushed their way to the bar where the elder Crump's son and Dickie's wine steward in waiting, Sweaty Crump, was serving feverishly. In the corner, Bob "Mittens" McGuire started to thump tunelessly on the battered old piano. Within seconds, he was pelted with slices of lemon and half-eaten sandwiches, and was hit smartly on the side of the head with a pickled egg, which stopped his playing.

He jumped to his feet and stared malevolently into the crowd, searching for the perpetrator. "My God," shouted someone, "if you were playing for shite Mittens, you'd never even smell it."

"Four pints of stout, Sweaty," Flanagan shouted over the din. "And pour four more, for these ones aren't going to touch the sides." Sweaty pulled four pints of the creamy ale and set them on the bar. Thirsty parked Pogo at the bar, grabbed one of the pints, and tilted it to his head. He poured it down his throat without swallowing, and then stood solemnly still as the crowd went quiet. Suddenly, he gripped the bar with both hands. "Steady as she goes there," said Flanagan, as Thirsty threw back his head and let fly with an ear-splitting ten-second burp that had the crowd cheering once more.

"Thirsty, you're just a natural athlete," Sweaty shouted as he handed him another pint. "How d'ya do that without vomiting?"

"It's a gift," replied Thirsty, as he took a huge swallow of the second pint and wiped his mouth on the sleeve of his battered jacket. "While you mention it, Sweaty, give us a half dozen of those pickled eggs, I hate throwing up on an empty stomach."

Across the street, and a little way up the hill, the tall figure of Sergeant James Finkter sat hunched over on a wooden three-legged stool by the bedroom window of his upstairs flat, above the Police Station. He stubbed out a filterless French cigarette in the ashtray with his yellowing fingers, and reached for a pair of binoculars. Finkter was the village's only law enforcement officer, and had long been frustrated over the complete and utter lack of action on his beat. Any trouble in this town was always dealt with by Uncle Dickie, long before it got anywhere near him, and he had had just about enough of it. As far as he was concerned, Uncle Dickie was responsible for bringing to Scroughtly exactly the kind of low-life scum that he detested the most. There were the caddies, for a start.

They were a bunch of cripples, queers, and drunken misfits, and the members were even worse, what with the Jews and that Pakistani, or whatever he was. He's a bloody Wog, Finkter thought. All the same, Paki or Indian or Sooty. All the bloody same, if you ask me. He looked through the binoculars, and focused on the Pig & Spigot. Some of the crowd had spilled outside, and were laughing and cheering and spilling their beer all over the street. Finkter sighed, and walked over to his bed-side table, where two candles provided the only light in the room, dimly illuminating the poster of the Queen Mother that hung over his bed. He ran his hands over his perfectly quaffed Prince Charles haircut, looked into the beautiful face of the progenitor of England's finest specimens, and clicked the heels of his shiny black boots together.

"Maybe tonight, Your highness," he whispered. "Maybe tonight." He pulled on his hat, grabbed his large flashlight and nightstick, blew out the candles, and made his way silently down the stairs and out the back door of the police station.

Outside the pub, Thirsty and Pogo were describing with great glee the events of the day and how, to a man, their players had outwitted the McGregors. Flanagan was waxing lyrical about Uncle Dickie's historic match with Hamish and repeating some of the old man's comeback lines, as Sergeant Finkter slipped across the street, some fifty yards farther up the hill. He slithered down the back alley, behind the Pig & Spigot, and took up a position below the pub, just within earshot of the group outside, which had now been joined by Herpy, and the two gay caddies, Mills and Boon.

"Public Intoxication," Finkter whispered to himself as he watched Boon unzip his pants and begin to pee against the wall of the pub. Finkter was beside himself with joy.

"And indecent exposure!" He pulled the nightstick out of his belt.

Further down the hill, Tweezer was pushing steadily upward toward the pub and could just pick out the shapes of his friends in the light that shone from the window, when suddenly a dark shape appeared between him and them. He stopped and put on his brake, fumbling in his pocket for a small flashlight. As the shadowy figure crept forward, tight to the wall, he flashed the tiny beam twice. Pogo was standing on his one real leg, and leaning on the other like a walking stick, raising his glass to drink, when the light caught his attention. Then, out of nowhere, Finkter appeared with his nightstick raised high, towering over the peeing Boon.

"OKAY, DIRTBAG!" he screamed, a look of orgiastic pleasure on his contorted face. "YOU'RE UNDER ARRESTAAAARGH!"

A large, hobnailed boot caught him flush in the middle of his face, driving his head back into the downspout behind him with a sickening clang. The boot, which had a leg attached to it, fell first, and was followed by Finkter, who crumpled into a heap against the wall and slid down, face first, into a puddle of

Charlie Boon's urine.

Tweezer released the brake, and rolled out of the darkness. "Hey, boys," he grinned. "How's it going?"

Flanagan looked at Finkter, and then at Pogo.

"Bugger me, Pogo," he said in amazement. "Did tha' just happen?"

Pogo took a long swallow from his glass, and bent down to pick up his leg. "Yeah," he said, matter-of-factly. "The old flying kick. Nobody sees it coming."

Boon zipped up his pants and looked down at the big policeman. He turned to his partner, Carson Mills, and said, "You know, Carson, you could be one of the Village People in that outfit. Look at the size of that truncheon!"

The caddies laughed, as Finkter groaned and stirred. Flanagan looked at his men and said, "Maybe we'd better get a keg, an' bugger off back to the caddieshack boys. Ah don't think we should be around when Officer Ectum here wakes up. Get everybody together, an' let's skedaddle."

Pogo hopped over beside Tweezer, and handed him a fresh pint from the windowsill.

"Thanks, pal," he said, as Tweezer drained it in one long draught.

Tweezer looked up from his chair, smiling. "No problem, Pogo," he said. "D'ya wanna lift back?"

Pogo swallowed the dregs of his pint, wiped his mouth on his sleeve, and said, "What's your record?"

Tweezer grinned. "One minute, seventeen seconds."

Pogo looked at his wristwatch. "Let's go for it!"

The caddies cheered as Tweezer spun his chair around, allowing Pogo to stuff his leg into the harness at the back. Pogo sat down in Tweezer's lap, putting his one large foot in between Tweezer's two smaller ones, and grasped the handlebars firmly. Thirsty stood in front of them and remarked, "This oughta be good, with only one real leg and two wheels between the two of you."

Flanagan counted them down. "Five, four, three, two, one!"

The wheelchair picked up speed rapidly, as Tweezer pumped his big triceps. They rattled down the cobbled street and disappeared into the darkness, urged on by the whoops and cheers of the crowd behind them.

It was dark. Tweezer had the nerves of the bomb disposal expert he had once been, and Pogo was scared. They hurtled down the hill toward the narrow entrance to Hadrian's Lane and the first real bend in the road. Tweezer's tangled mop of brown hair was beating against his ears as he shouted at Pogo, who had a death grip on the handlebars. "This is great!" he yelled over the roar of the wind. "I've never had an airbag before!"

"Oh, shite," Pogo gasped as they hit the corner.

"Lean with me, Pogo!" Tweezer shouted, as the two men twisted their torsos to the right. The wheelchair lurched onto its right wheel and they shot around the corner into a dip in the road where, for a moment, both wheels left the ground. Then they crested the hill and Pogo left Tweezer's lap for a split-second before they landed and bounced into the home straight.

"Tuck!" Tweezer shouted, as they whizzed past the entrance to Gussett Hall, and a few seconds later, they hurtled into the

gravel parking lot of the club. Tweezer pulled on the brake, and the chair skidded to a halt with inches to spare between Pogo's nose and the wooden wall of the caddieshack. Tweezer looked at his watch. "Yess!" he shouted. "One minute, fourteen!"

Back up the hill, Herpy appeared from the pub, rolling a keg of beer in front of him. "Right," said Flanagan. "Let's go see how they did!"

A few moments later, the old yellow Volkswagen, stuffed to the roof with caddies, set off down the hill, a little more slowly.

CHAPTER SIX

Bertie Crump hummed quietly to himself as he cleaned up the tables in the card room. The only member remaining was the giant figure of Reggie Carstairs, who lay slumped in his armchair in the corner, snoring like a rhino. He stirred slightly at the clink of glasses as Crump loaded them onto his tray, and when the first ray of sunlight burst through the twisted Venetian blinds, it caught him right across the eyelids. He snorted, rubbed his eyes, and slowly pulled himself upright.

"Bloody hell," he groaned, looking around the room. He spotted Crump. "Crump," he bellowed. "Did you put a turd in my mouth when I was sleeping?"

"No, sir, I believe that would probably be your tongue."

Reggie smacked his lips. "Well, it tastes like a turd," he said. "Bring me a large glass of orange juice and call me a ambulance, there's a good fellow."

Holding the tray of glasses in front of him, Crump backed through the swinging doors into the kitchen and returned a few moments later with a tall glass of orange juice.

"Here you are, sir," he smiled. "And you're an ambulance."

"Ha, ha, Crump," shouted Carstairs. "Bloody good show," as he drained the glass. "Now, where are the rest of those buggers?"

"They all hit the wall sir, and most of them made it only as far as the Dormy House, but I doubt if any of them are up yet," Crump replied.

"Well, it's about bloody time they were," said Carstairs, as he heaved his huge bulk out of the chair. He hobbled off down the hallway, past the portraits and the trophy case, but stopped suddenly when he heard a loud scrunching noise under his feet. Slowly, he looked down and then back up to the trophy case. About a square foot of the glass was missing, as was the ancient wooden box that contained the digit.

"Holy mackerel!" he yelled. "Someone has pinched the digit." Then, like a giant bowling ball, he set off down the hallway. He burst out through the front door and thundered down the wooden veranda steps, which squeaked and groaned under his vast weight. He set off across the gravel to the Dormy House.

"Gussett! Gussett! Dickie, old boy!" he yelled, as he burst through the door, and made his way between the beds, with their sleeping occupants slowly coming to life. Major Norma Oglesby was first up, great clumps of gray chest hair sprouting over the neckline of her pink chiffon nightdress, as she swung her legs over the edge of her bed.

"Reggie," he said. "What the devil is going on?"

"Oglesby, the most dreadful thing has happened," puffed Carstairs. "Someone has stolen the digit."

An atmosphere of urgency enveloped the room as the rest of the members realized the seriousness of the situation.

"Stolen the digit?" Oglesby asked incredulously. "Y-y-y-y-y-yes," stammered Carstairs, when suddenly the door at the end of the dormitory was flung open and Uncle Dickie strode into the room, his eyes blazing. The room was silent as he slowly walked across the Persian carpet to Carstairs.

"Show me," he said quietly. "Oglesby, go over to Beamish's quarters and tell him to come to my office immediately."

"Of course, Dickie," said Oglesby as she pulled a huge floral kimono from the drawer of her nightstand. She struggled into it, and hurried after Carstairs and Uncle Dickie.

Stanley Beamish had been Uncle Dickie's butler, it seemed, since the day he was born. Like anyone who really knew Major General Sir Richard Gussett, Beamish adored him and had more than once risked his life for his master, both in wartime and in peace. Once, in occupied France, having lost his weapon, he had run full-tilt from his foxhole, and head-butted an oncoming Panzer tank. This was a gesture so pointless that it had confused the German tank driver just long enough for one of Uncle Dickie's men to draw a bead just under the turret with his bazooka and knock it out.

Unfortunately for Beamish, a piece of shrapnel had ripped off his left testicle in the same incident. Undeterred, the valiant Beamish, in the absence of a proper prosthesis, had set about whittling a new one out of the stock of a captured German Mauser and had stitched it up himself. "Only a scratch, Major," he was reported to have said. A severe attack of woodworm had later necessitated the removal of his handiwork, and since that day, he had been known to his friends as, "Half-a-Bag Beamish."

Stanley had chosen to spend the evening before the theft of the digit at the Pig & Spigot in the company of the Scrought's Wood caddies and, at the time that Major Norma Oglesby shook him into consciousness, was in an alcohol-induced coma. When he came to, the first thing he noticed was that his shoulders were being gripped by a huge, bald, fart-breathing woman with a handlebar mustache and yellowing teeth. Understandably, Half-a-Bag Beamish thought he had died, gone to hell, and bumped into his estranged wife, who was the reason he had joined the armed forces in the first place.

He let out a bloodcurdling, high-pitched squeal of terror, and rocketed back under his bed sheets, from where he started to sob uncontrollably.

"Beamish, you idiot," yelled Major Oglesby. "Come out from under there. I need you!"

"No, no," wailed Stanley. "For the love of God, Ethel. Mr. Floppy can't go to Squidgy Town any more."

"What the bloody hell are you jabbering about, man?" said Oglesby. "Just get your clothes on and be in Sir Dickie's office in five minutes, and that's an order."

Stanley winced as the door slammed and it was a few moments before he found the courage to stick his head out from underneath the sheets. He looked nervously around the room and slumped back onto his pillow. "What a nightmare," he wheezed. Thirty seconds later, he was fast asleep again.

Uncle Dickie and Carstairs hurried across the gravel and were climbing the veranda steps, when suddenly Uncle Dickie stopped and bent over. The members, many of whom were following in pajamas and bare feet, gathered around. "What is it, Dickie?" asked the Maharajah, who was not yet wearing his turban. His long, silvery hair hung over his thin brown shoulders and down to his waist.

Uncle Dickie stood up holding a small cluster of brown pellets between his thumb and forefinger. He squeezed them together, sniffed, and then threw them to the ground, pulling out a linen handkerchief from his trouser pocket. "Sheep shit," he growled, wiping his hands. "And it stinks of McGregor, or my arse is parsley."

"Forgive me," started the Maharajah. "But I have seen your arse and parsley, too, and it would seem to me, my old friend, that they are entirely dissimilar."

"Indeed they are, Poony old boy," said Uncle Dickie, gravely, as he turned to face the members. "Indeed they are." He drew a deep breath. "My friends, I have always been proud of you all, but never more so than yesterday when we claimed back from the evil McGregors that which is rightfully ours. Now, in typically underhanded fashion, they have stolen it once more. I promise you all this day that I shall bring it back and the soul of Sir Basil shall sleep peacefully once more."

"Aye," piped up Rabbi Hannigan, or my willie's a knish."

"I have seen your willie," said the Maharajah, "and a knish, too, and believe me—"

"Yes, yes we know," said Uncle Dickie, waving him down. "Let's get to business. Everyone get dressed and meet in the bar at eight sharp."

Meanwhile, fifteen miles away in Nerdlington, the first northern-bound train of the morning was about to leave the station.

"No, no, no, ye dinnae understand," said Hamish McGregor. "She's like a member of the family, ye know, like a wee pet."

"It's a bloody sheep," said the stationmaster, licking the end of his pencil, and thumbing through a small booklet. "And live-stock are specifically prohibited from traveling in the passenger cars under Bylaw Thirty-Eight, Subsection C, Paragraph Three of the Railway Code. Here," he said, shoving the small grubby pamphlet under Hamish's nose with a sarcastic smirk, "Read it and bleat."

Brenna jerked back on her leash as the train wheezed and hissed. She didn't care where McGregor intended for her to go, as long as it wasn't anywhere near the huge metal monster to her left.

Hamish reached down and fondled the animal's neck. "Easy there, lassie," he whispered. Then suddenly he grabbed the stationmaster by the necktie and pulled him close.

"Listen, you pompous English pillock," he hissed. "Unless you want to have that wee rulebook shoved right up your blow-hole, you'll let me and my girl on the train right now, okay?"

Brenna, sensing the moment was right, suddenly shot off up the platform, jerking the leash from McGregor's hand; and, as fast as her three legs would take her, she disappeared down the ramp, headed across the track in front of the locomotive, and down the other side of the train.

"Brenna!" screamed McGregor, dropping the stationmaster into a crumpled heap. He grabbed his duffle bag and set off after the sheep just as the train started to move. Still in great pain, he cut in front and down the other side as fast as his wounds would allow. The frightened animal had frozen as the train started down the track and Hamish quickly caught up with her. Swiftly, he tossed her over his shoulder and grasped the door handle of the slow-moving carriage, swinging the door open and heaving himself, along with Brenna, into the train.

Uncle Dickie paced the Persian carpet in his office, while the Maharajah sat in a large, burgundy leather armchair, rolling a Turkish cigarette. "What bothers me Poony, old boy, is, I will have to send Beamish up north to survey this damned golf course. Now where the devil is he?"

The Maharajah stood up, flicked open an old brass Zippo, and lit up. A cloud of perfumed smoke billowed in front of his face and surrounded his turban as he walked toward the bay window.

Maharajah Poonsavvy had been Uncle Dickie's closest friend since their boyhood days in India, where Uncle Dickie's father had been stationed for several years. Jahindir Poonsavvy was the son of an incredibly wealthy Indian merchant, and many of Uncle Dickie's earliest memories were of elephant rides and tiger hunts with his young friend. When the Regiment left India, Uncle Dickie found himself back in England, seemingly with little chance of ever seeing Jahindir again; but a few months later, he was overjoyed to see the slim, turban-clad boy join him and his classmates at Eton. Jahindir was now a Maharajah himself, his father having been killed by a tiger, which left the boy orphaned but fantastically wealthy. His school holidays were spent at Gussett Hall, where the two boys became inseparable.

After the Maharajah graduated, he decided not to return to his homeland because the Muslim religion forbade him to take part in certain activities of which he had become rather fond during his time in England. He had become partial to both women and alcohol. Tall and slender, he had a perfectly trimmed handlebar mustache, and without his turban, his silver hair spilled all the way to his waist. He was already an inveterate womanizer, with as many as ten women on a string at any one time. For a while he lived in London, where he still kept a lavish apartment, but the toil of having to keep track of so many affairs at one time eventually drove Poonsavvy toward the calm and solitude of Scrought's Wood. There, he had become equally obsessed with the game of golf.

"I can't remember which started to wear out first, my willie or my mind," he would say to Uncle Dickie. "I'm not as good as I once was, but I'm as good once as I ever was."

The Maharajah stood at the bay window of the clubhouse and looked out across the gravel car park toward Beamish's cottage. Stanley was trudging slowly toward the clubhouse, wearing the crumpled shirt and trousers he'd had on the night before. He ran his hand through his unruly haystack of salt-and-pepper hair, yawned, and scratched his backside, when a small tan-and-white blur shot out from under the veranda and instantly attached itself to his left leg.

He let out a yell of surprise and tried to shake Dwilby off, but the little terrier had a good grip and was humping his leg ferociously. Unwisely, he reached down and tried to pry the dog off, receiving a nasty nip on the hand for his trouble. Then Stanley began to hop around in a circle, trying in vain to shake the dog loose.

"There he is," said the Maharajah, pointing a long, tawny

finger at the scene outside. Uncle Dickie strode over to stand beside Poonsavvy, and bent over to slide up the old wooden sash window frame. He stuck his head out.

"Beamish, you idiot," he yelled. "Stand still and let him finish or you'll lose a finger."

At the sound of the Major General's voice, Stanley stood rigidly to attention and saluted, as the dog continued to pound relentlessly on his calf. "Yes, sir," he barked. Uncle Dickie withdrew back into the room and pulled the window closed.

"That damn dog," he sighed. "Sometimes I think it's in charge here. I'd have the randy little bugger gelded myself if it weren't for the wrath of Agnes Flanagan that would surely follow."

Some moments later, there was a tap on the door and a decidedly disheveled-looking Stanley Beamish sidled into Uncle Dickie's office. "Ah, Beamish," smiled Uncle Dickie. "How was it for you?"

Beamish straightened up and stood to attention. "I have to admit I feel a little violated, sir," he said. "Something should be done about that dog."

"Yes, I know," said Uncle Dickie. "I wouldn't expect a phone call or flowers either. But anyway, Beamish, more to the point, I have a little job for you, just like old times."

Beamish grinned boyishly. "You mean," he said, tapping the side of his nose, "undercover, sir?"

"Exactly," said Uncle Dickie, rising from his chair. He walked around the old mahogany desk and clapped both his hands onto Beamish's shoulders.

"The McGregors stole the digit last night, and you and I, my faithful old friend, are going to get it back. I need you to go on a reconnaissance mission. I want you to fly to Edinburgh and then head north to the Tay Club, scout the territory, and map out the yardage and hazards to find out what's going on."

Beamish swallowed hard and giggled nervously. "You want me to fly, sir?" he stammered.

"Yes, said Uncle Dickie. "I know you aren't fond of the experience, but time is of the essence here, and we must simply get the jump on the McGregors. They'll no doubt be traveling over land, because of that beastly goat of theirs, so this way you can be there before they arrive."

"B-b-but sir, I get airsick on a thick rug," Beamish replied. "You know what happened last time I flew with you."

"Yes," smiled Uncle Dickie, "but to the best of my knowledge the airlines don't fly upside down too often; so this time, the excrement will run down your trouser legs instead out of your collar. Now run along. There's a ticket waiting for you at the airport at Newcastle-upon-Tyne."

Beamish straightened up once more, saluted, and said, less than enthusiastically, "Yes, sir." He did an about-turn, headed for the door, and stopped to pick up an old sand wedge that was leaning against the wall. "May I, sir? " he asked.

"But of course, old boy," beamed Uncle Dickie. "Just hold it by the head and whack the little bugger with the grip if he comes near you."

The Maharajah and Uncle Dickie watched from the bay window as Beamish, brandishing the club above his head, tiptoed down the steps and bolted across the gravel to his cottage.

"That man has the strength of ten men and the heart of lion, Poony," said Uncle Dickie fondly.

"Oh, yes," replied the Maharajah, taking a long draw on his cigarette. "And the brain of a walnut."

CHAPTER SEVEN

S ergeant James Finkter was staring at his reflection in the mirror, and it was not a pretty sight. His recollection of the previous evening's events was a little clouded, to say the least, and he had absolutely no idea what had hit him. In fact, Pogo's boot had caught him square on the nose, which was obviously broken, his lower lip was split inside his mouth, and he had a nasty gash on the back of his head from the edge of the downspout. He flicked on an electric razor, and started to carefully shave his face, and his perfectly formed royal family regulation sideburns, or at least the parts of them that weren't broken. Earlier, he had taken his urine-stained uniform out back and burned it, not wanting to take the risk of infecting his washing machine, or corrupting any other articles of his clothing that might have come into contact with it.

He finished shaving and stood back to admire his handiwork. Tufts of black bristles sprouted from under his nostrils, which were grotesquely squashed and swollen, and his bottom lip also had a dark shadow to match the bruising.

"Bastards," he muttered. "Filthy rotten bastards, every last one of them."

Seething and barely able to control himself, he put on his spare uniform, and made his way down the stairs, and into the little office that was the police station. He sat down behind his desk, and stared out through the yellowing net curtains into the main street, where life went on as usual in Scroughtly. Morons, he thought. Walking past his window, meaningless little people with their dismal little lives, in this stinking little town. He hammered his fist down on the desk, screamed, "BASTARDS!" at the top of his voice, and stood up suddenly, sending the chair skidding across the linoleum floor, where it collided with a small table with a fishbowl on top. The table rocked precariously, almost toppling the bowl, which sloshed water and a small orange fish out onto the floor.

Finkter freaked at the sight of the fish flipping and wiggling.

"Princess Di!" he gasped, dropping to his knees and fumbling for the little creature, which squirted out of his fingertips several times before he was able to get it back into the bowl. He drew a deep breath, pulled the chair back in front of the desk, and sat down heavily. He had to pull himself together, but he felt so violated and so helpless; that was the problem. Everything and everyone in this village was controlled by Uncle Dickie, and yet *he*, Sergeant James Finkter, was supposed to be the law. No one gave him any respect, the arseholes. They whispered behind his back whenever he was around and they were always sniggering at his stupid name. What in God's name, he thought, were my parents thinking about, when they named me James, with a surname like Finkter? He'd heard every possible variation, Officer Ectum, Inspector Anus, Constable Colon, The Bumhole Bobby, etc. He put his elbows on the desk, held his head in his hands, buried his fingertips into the sockets of his eyes, and groaned as he rubbed them. The old black rotary phone on his desk rang, scaring him rigid. He grabbed the receiver.

"Yes," he snapped. "What is it?"

"Is this Sergeant Finkter?" a silky baritone voice asked.

"Yes, it is," barked Finkter. "What do you want?"

"Sergeant James Finkter?" enquired the voice, deliberately running the "s" of James into the "f" of Finkter. Finkter held the receiver in front of his face, looked at it murderously, and returned it to his ear.

"Look, pal, I've heard it all before," he said. "If you have something to say, then say it, or I will have this line traced, and—"

"Hold on there, old boy," the voice cut in smoothly. "Before this day is over, I expect that you and I will be friends. Does the phrase 'The enemy of my enemy is my friend,' mean anything to you at all?"

Finkter looked blank for a few seconds. Nope, he thought. That doesn't mean anything to me.

"You're not from around here, are you?" he asked.

"Indeed I'm not," said the stranger. "But I shall be in the Black Swan in a few moments' time. Perhaps we could meet. I have a proposition for you."

Finkter lowered the handset, took a deep breath, and pursed his lips. This had possibilities. A clandestine meeting with a mysterious, well-spoken stranger, he thought. It could lead to actual police work. "I'll meet you there," he whispered, looking over his shoulder, and around the office to the front door. "But how will I recognize you?"

"It's seven-thirty in the morning, you dolt," the voice said, a little impatiently. "I imagine we'll be the only ones there. Come around back, and Mr. Mellon will let you in."

Finkter put the phone down, and made his way back upstairs,

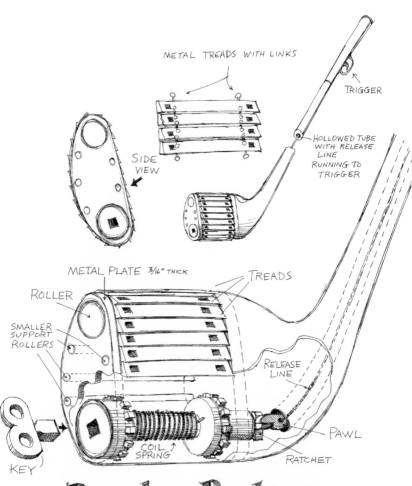

METAL TREADS WITH LINKS

TRIGGER

HOLLOWED TUBE WITH RELEASE LINE RUNNING TO TRIGGER

SIDE VIEW

METAL PLATE 3/16" THICK

TREADS

ROLLER

SMALLER SUPPORT ROLLERS

RELEASE LINE

PAWL

KEY

COIL SPRING

RATCHET

Bungley Back-up

The Bungley backup wedge (Bungley, Sir Thomas. *1911.*)

The Bungley wedge was an expert's club, used by only the very low handicap player, due to the disastrous consequences of a mistimed shot. The deeply grooved face was constructed in a separate piece from the rest of the head, and was attached not unlike a modern garage door. The position of the face was set by a strong metal spring, and the tension was controlled by turning a key, which was inserted into a hole in the toe. The entire mechanism of this remarkable club was triggered by a wire, attached to a metal ring, which the player wore on the index finger of the lower hand on the grip. At the exact moment of impact, the trigger was pulled, sending the face downward, biting into the ball, and imparting incredible amounts of backspin. Only two of these clubs were ever made, due to the untimely death of Sir Thomas, who was killed in 1917 by a piece of flying metal, in an overtensioning incident at Royal St. Georges, Kent. His last words, as he lay bleeding to death just short of the fifteenth green were, "Fuck me, but that hurt."

where he checked his face one more time in the mirror. He still looked like someone had kicked him in the face with a very large boot. He picked up his domed helmet from the nightstand, eased it painfully on over the crown of his swollen head, loosened the chinstrap a little, and straightened his jaw. A few moments later, he slipped out the back entrance to the police station, and made his way through the little garden, past the smoldering remains of his best uniform. He skulked up the alley, over the hill, and down to the back entrance of the Black Swan.

In the caddieshack, Flanagan had his hands clasped behind his back, and was pacing backward and forward, as Herpy and Pogo played cards in the corner. Thirsty sucked on a bottle of red wine, and wiped his mouth on his sleeve.

"Wassup, Seamus?" he asked. "You look like there's something bothering you."

"Aye, there is, wee man," answered Flanagan, stopping at the window and pointing a finger at the clubhouse. "There's somethin' smelly goin' on here, wi' the digit disappearin' an everything. Party or no party, the Major would never let such a thing happen. He's just too sharp fer tha'."

Thirsty burped, and stared vacantly into space. "Aye, I know what y'mean, but there was a few of them that weren't too sharp last night. Crump said half of the members went tits up in the dining room at four o'clock this morning. None of them would've heard a thing."

Flanagan sat down on the windowsill and turned to Thirsty. "Maybe they weren't meant to hear anything," he said thoughtfully.

Auntie Myrtle was watering a large potted Yucca in the conservatory when she heard the regimental click of her husband's heels on the marble. Uncle Dickie swept dramatically into the room.

"My dear," he said gravely, "the most dreadful thing has happened."

"Really, darling," Aunt Myrtle said. "Let me guess. Poultice the cat has shredded your best long johns, and you are going to beat him to death with that golf club under your arm. You know, the one you only bring out on special occasions."

Startled, Uncle Dickie looked at the Bungley wedge as if it had been planted on him, shifted nervously and leaned the club against the wall. "Er, no, my precious, you see the digit has been stolen, and I fear it's the work of the McGregors. Something will have to be done."

Auntie Myrtle straightened, and looked with amusement at her husband, who was doing his level best to look indignant, but was reddening visibly above his collar.

"What?" Uncle Dickie asked. "This is serious, Myrtle, I mean…"

"I know, I know," Auntie Myrtle said. "The fossilized finger of the patron saint of Scotland is missing. However will the poor old ghost pick his saintly schnozz?"

Uncle Dickie's shoulders slumped in resignation. He had never been able to slide one by his wife.

"Yes, well," he started.

Auntie Myrtle smiled and walked gracefully over to where he stood, rocking back and forth on his heels, with his arms folded in front of him. She cupped his reddening face in her hands and kissed him on the end of his nose.

"Go on, then," she said. "I'm sure you have things to do!"

Like an eight-year-old on Christmas morning, Uncle Dickie wrapped his arms around her, a sheepish grin spreading across his face.

"Thanks awfully, Myrtle," he chirped, spinning on his heel, and heading for the front door, pausing only to grab the Bungley wedge on the way. "I'll see you for supper!"

Smiling and shaking her head, Auntie Myrtle went back to her plants.

Stanley Beamish was talking to himself, as he rummaged through his chest of drawers, looking for a British Rail timetable.

"If there's a nonstop, I'll get there just as quick as flying," he muttered, throwing a ball of string over his shoulder, and pushing aside a dog-eared copy of *Big 'n' Bouncy*.

Stanley had always been a nervous flyer, but his last venture skyward had convinced him that he would never, ever, under any circumstances, do it again. The occasion had been Auntie Myrtle's seventieth birthday, when Uncle Dickie had decided he wanted to write "I LOVE YOU" in giant letters in the skies over Gussett Hall. Stanley had been in charge of holding the smoke canister, as Uncle Dickie performed a complicated series of loops and barrel rolls in his ancient Sopwith Camel. The message that Stanley had squirted in the sky was illegible, and in truth, as Flanagan had said afterward, "It was easier to read the trail of vomit on the ground."

"Here it is," Stanley shouted joyfully, dropping to his knees. He thumbed through the little book, stopping at, "Newcastle-upon-Tyne to Edinburgh," and ran his index finger feverishly down the list of arrival times. As luck would have it, there was a nonstop leaving in two hours' time, which meant he might just make it, if he really got a move on. He grabbed a small leather bag from under the bed and tossed in a pair of brass knuckles, a one-man pup tent, his field glasses and helmet, a toothbrush, a half-empty bottle of Bushmills, a folder of maps, and his old sleeping bag. He was packed. A few moments later, he was running down the drive toward Scroughtly, and the 9:30 A.M. bus to Newcastle-upon Tyne.

Meanwhile, on the first train from Nerdlington, Hamish had made himself and Brenna comfortable in one of the compartments. There were two bench seats facing each other, and he had seated himself facing forward, with Brenna between his legs and partially hidden underneath his kilt. Hamish was exhausted and had almost drifted off to sleep with his head against the window, when there was a knock on the door and a small Japanese man with a bowler hat, a rolled-up umbrella, and a briefcase slid the door back and entered the compartment.

"Hurro," said the little man, bowing politely and doffing his hat. "Awfurry preased to meet you, my name is…"

But that was as far as he got. Brenna, who had been dozing

with her head between Hamish's legs, had heard the stranger's voice and stirred slightly, causing Hamish's sporran to rise up about three or four inches. The man looked down and noticed a small woolly tail swish backward and forward on the floor, underneath the bench.

Hamish smiled evilly, and waved his hand. "Hurro to you, too," he said, as the stranger backed out of the compartment, his hat still in hand.

As the countryside clacked and hummed hypnotically past his face, tufts of green and beige grass melted into gray stone walls and the thick red hair hanging over Hamish's forehead dampened the vibration from the windowpane, lulling him into a deep sleep. As the train rolled into Newcastle and lurched to a stop, he awoke, in plenty of time to catch the next nonstop to Edinburgh.

Stanley climbed off the bus and hurried down the steps to the train station. He glanced anxiously at his watch.

"Bollocks," he muttered nervously. He had only five minutes to spare and all the beer he had guzzled and the greasy food he had devoured the previous evening had left him with stomach cramps. On the long bus journey, he had endured many painful waves and now it looked like he didn't have time for a pit stop if he were to make the train. He stood outside the ticket window, shifting uncomfortably from one foot to the other, as he bought a one-way ticket to Edinburgh, and he was hurrying down the platform toward the train when he was hit by a particularly agonizing spasm. He slowed down and tried to ride it out, but this was one of those times when it looked like a man was going to have to make a decision. Stanley was positive that a half-decent fart would alleviate the pain he felt in his stomach. But what if he was wrong, he thought, and he let fly with a flock of sparrows?

Even though he knew that this was going to be one of those defining moments in the life of his underwear, Stanley felt he had no choice but to go for it. Later, he described his ill-conceived gamble like this:

"If I had been sitting on the toilet, I would have hit everything except the water."

For Stanley, this was clearly a disaster, and now he was faced with a seemingly insurmountable problem. The train was hissing and wheezing, and was about to leave for Edinburgh. By choosing not to fly, he had, for the first time in his life, disobeyed an order from Uncle Dickie; and, in order to cover his tracks, he had to make this train. The problem was, he was about ten more paces from making *actual* tracks, and all he could see to his right was a little platform shop selling newspapers, candy, and novelties. On the off chance that for once in his life he might get lucky, he shuffled bandy-legged into the store, where to his amazement, he saw cheap sweatsuits for sale in plastic bags. Pants and a sweatshirt, for only ten pounds! Hastily, he rummaged in his wallet, pulled out a ten-pound note, and tossed it at the assistant, who was looking at him oddly. He nodded gratefully, grabbed a plastic bag, and shuffled out to the train, which was just starting to roll out of the station. He swung himself on board, and made a beeline for the nearest toilet, where he slammed the door behind him.

Stanley drew a huge sigh of relief, and began to undress in the tiny room, starting by kicking off his shoes. This was so unusual, he thought, to catch a lucky break like this. He pulled down his trousers, which were in even worse shape than he had imagined, and carefully removed his underwear. Then he pulled down the sliding window, and—using the clothing he had removed and a whole roll of toilet tissue—he cleaned himself up as best as he could. Finally, he threw both the soiled garments out the window of the moving train, and ripped open the plastic bag.

"Oh my god!" Outside, the passengers heard a muffled scream.

Naturally, the bag contained only a sweatshirt.

A few carriages further down the train, Hamish sat behind the *Daily Telegraph*, which was covering Brenna completely. He wore a pair of half-moon spectacles low on his thin beaky nose and was pretending to read, as the train picked up speed. Out of the corner of his eye, he noticed a strange figure enter the compartment. A large man, wearing a grubby white button-down shirt, tucked into what appeared to be an upside-down red sweatshirt, was looking for somewhere to sit down. Hamish looked at him more closely. The man had forced his legs into the armholes of the sweatshirt, and tied it around his waist with a belt. He was holding the neck hole closed with one hand, and had a small leather bag in the other, as he walked down the aisle, looking for a vacant seat. Hamish raised the paper higher as Stanley approached.

"Ahem," Stanley coughed quietly. "Would you mind if I sat here?"

"Please yerself," said Hamish, still hidden behind the paper.

Stanley sat down heavily and shoved his bag under the seat. A few moments later, his head lolled to one side, and he drifted off. Hamish lowered the paper, just enough so he could squint over the top. He stared at Stanley, knowing he had seen this man somewhere before. He watched, as Stanley snorted, and lost his grip on the neckline of his sweatshirt.

Stanley's bat and ball flopped out onto the Naugahyde seat, much to the consternation of the elderly lady sitting opposite him. She shrieked, Hamish raised his newspaper, and, for Stanley Beamish, all hell broke loose one more time.

The Edinburgh express made one unscheduled stop that day, leaving Stanley, a tragic figure, on the platform at Snartley-on-Sea. He stood there with his heels together and his toes pointed out, all white calves, black socks, and red sweatshirt, holding his leather bag and watching the faces slide past as the train left the station. In the third-to-last carriage, there was one big red-bearded face stuck to the window, a face that dragged Stanley's eyeballs with it, until the train was around the corner and out of sight. Recognition hit Stanley like a slap in the face, as his eyes faced front once more:

It was that arsehole Hamish McGregor. Stanley turned his head to face front once more, and found himself looking at one of the small back gardens of a row of terraced houses on the other side of the tracks, and a clothesline, heavy with pants and shirts that were fluttering in the breeze. He jumped down onto the track and clambered through a wire fence into the garden. He took a pair of jeans and a gray flannel shirt off the line. Then he tore off his sweatshirt, pulled on the jeans and the shirt, and set off between the walls of the terraced houses toward the main street of the village. But suddenly he stopped and looked skyward. He shook his head, reached into his bag, and pulled out his wallet. Stanley's face was dark and his brow furrowed, as he walked back to the clothesline, where he pegged up two ten-pound notes. Then he made his way through the garden and into the main street of the village. "Hamish bloody McGregor," he muttered to himself as he walked quickly toward the nearest pub.

All his life, Stanley had been the butt of other people's jokes, and the smirk of triumph on McGregor's face as the train had rolled by had really hurt. Stanley resolved that this was one smirk too many. He, Stanley Beamish, was going to wipe it off the ugly orange face of Hamish McGregor. This time, the smirk would be his. He walked into the pub, where a few locals were sitting, sipping at warm beers, and chatting.

"I need to rent a car," he announced loudly. A few heads turned, and an elderly man behind the bar slipped off his stool and walked around to stand in front of Stanley. He looked him up and down, with a curious expression on his face.

"How much have ye got?" he said.

Stanley emptied his wallet onto the table in front of him, and sorted through the money. "I have exactly two hundred forty-seven pounds and seventeen pence," he said proudly.

The bartender sifted through the notes, and pushed a pile back to Stanley.

"Ah'll take two hundred pounds, and if ye bring it back in one piece, ye can have one hundred pounds back."

"Fair enough," said Stanley, "Where is it?"

The bartender felt in his pocket and pulled out a single British Leyland key. "It's red, and it's in front of number Twenty-two, down the street to your left."

"Thanks," said Stanley. "I'll look after it for you."

Stanley headed back out the door of the pub and the bartender returned to his stool, where he folded the wad of notes in half and shoved them into his jacket pocket. One of the locals, an old herring-boat captain called Alec who had watched the whole transaction, looked at him quizzically and asked, "Why did ye do tha', Bob?"

Bob stared back and rubbed the gray stubble on his chin thoughtfully.

"Well, he was wearin' mah jeans an mah shirt already, Alec, so ah thought, Why not?"

Stanley stopped outside number 22 and realized that this was the house whose clothesline he had robbed a few moments earlier. In the front room he noticed a little gray-haired lady in a housecoat, waving his ten-pound notes at him and smiling. He smiled back nervously, waved, and looked at the car. It was a bright red Mini Cooper, and not in bad shape, either. He opened the door, and squeezed behind the wheel, reaching underneath the seat to let it back as far as it would go. He turned the key, and the little four-cylinder engine snarled into life first time. With another cheery wave to the old lady in the front room, Stanley engaged first gear, and let the clutch out. With a chirp of the front tires, Stanley's head snapped back as the car shot off down the main street at an alarming rate. He flew past the front door of the pub, where a few of the locals had gathered to watch. Stanley had the little car in second gear by this time, but he was too shocked to take either hand off the steering wheel to wave at anyone, as the car continued to accelerate rapidly.

"It's pretty quick, tha' thing, Bob," said Alec, as they watched Stanley disappear around the corner at the bottom of the street.

"Och, aye," the bartender said, sipping on his pint. "My son rallies them, you know. Says it goes from Good Heavens to Fuck Me in about four seconds."

Alec looked down the street. "By the look on tha' fella's face, ah think it got to Fuck Me even quicker than tha'."

CHAPTER EIGHT

Outside the main train station in Edinburgh, Gregor McGregor waited impatiently beside the old truck. Shuggie was in the passenger seat, looking at his wristwatch.

"Where the bloody hell is he, Gregor?" he whined. "Tha' train wis supposed tae be in here twenty minutes ago, an I'm starvin'."

Gregor looked back menacingly. "Shuggie," he said. "If ah were you, an' believe me, ah'm glad ah'm not, ah would be disinclined to mention mah belly when Hamish shows up."

Shuggie looked hurt. "Ooh, all right then, Slimbo," he said sniffily. "Ah forgot tha' yer body is a temple, an' the thought of sustenance nivver crosses yer mind... Not that it wud be a long journey, of course."

"Shut up, you!" hissed Gregor. "Here he comes!"

Hamish was walking toward the truck with Brenna on a tight leash and a grim expression on his face. He reached into his duffel bag, brought out a wooden box, and broke into a broad grin, as he held it high above his head.

"She's back, boys," he yelled. Gregor ran to meet him with open arms, and Shuggie tumbled out of the cab, smiling broadly. He joined the two brothers in a group hug and said, "Tha's great, Hamish. Well done!"

Hamish tied Brenna down securely in the back of the truck and jumped up into the driver's seat. Gregor climbed in from the other side, followed by Shuggie, whose enormous bulk squeezed Hamish and Gregor together so tight that Hamish felt the driver's door might burst open and eject him into the street. They hadn't gotten fifty yards from the curb, when Shuggie said, "Hamish, can we stop at McDonald's on the way hame?"

Brenna was glad to have someone that size, and that warm, to snuggle up against on the way home.

It was only right and fitting that a direct descendant of Brother Dick should be so involved in the battle for the honor of the greatest game on earth. Stanley, of course, was completely unaware that his lineage could be traced through the ancient records of the Parish of St. Mungo directly to Gertrude, daughter of Desmond the Disturbing. All Stanley knew was that he had been born and raised in Scroughtly and that his father had run away when he was eight months old. Apart from the times that he had been fighting under the command of Uncle Dickie, who had always looked after him and his mother, he had lived in Scroughtly all his life.

As he gripped the wheel of the little red car, he was consumed by the desire to be through Dundee and on the northern side of the Tay estuary in as much time or less than it would have taken if he had flown into Edinburgh and rented a car. The needle on the speedometer was waving around wildly between 90 and 100 mph as he weaved in and out of traffic, his right foot flat to the floor. Stanley was on a mission again, he was wearing pants again, and he was starting to enjoy himself.

The Mini Cooper was remarkably fast and stuck to the road like glue, and Stanley, who had learned to drive at high speed on desert roads in various military vehicles, soon got used to the little car's understeer. He sped into the corners, braking as late as he could as the car drifted straight ahead and then gunned it out of the apex, swinging the tail back into line. With one stop for fuel, he was back on schedule by late afternoon, and slowed to a tourist-like tootle once he had gotten through Dundee and had the Tay on his right. He made his way through Carnoustie and on out the coast a few miles, parked at the side of the road, and pulled a crumpled ordinance survey map and a compass out of his bag. He spread the map out over the hood of the car and pored over it. The engine popped and clicked as it cooled, and there was a sudden chill in the air as the sun began to dip below the hills behind him.

"Yes!" Stanley shouted triumphantly. "The McGregor compound is exactly two and one quarter miles that way!"

He spun around on his heels and pointed a finger straight out into the North Sea, directly toward Denmark.

"Shite!"

Stanley turned to his right and looked across the firth at the dark shadows of an old gray town, scratching his head. The setting sun glinted off the steel-blue water as he picked up the map, and, holding it like a newspaper, started deciphering to himself.

"Now, if that's St. Andrews, which would be south," he said, nodding across the water, "then I must be here…

"Upside down and in South Wales, if that map is anything to go by," said a loud voice behind him.

It was Hamish, and behind him were most of the clan, all of whom were wearing broad grins.

"Hullo, Half-a-Bag," Hamish said cheerfully, putting his arm around Stanley's shoulder and pointing a finger at the map.

"You see? There's Cardiff, and there's Porthcawl, which has a golf club, filled with toffee-nosed old wankers like your precious Uncle Dickie and his senile friends, hasn't it?"

Stanley stood silent, mortified and furious, as Hamish snatched the map from him.

"Grab him, lads," Hamish ordered. He turned to look at the car. "And push that wee jam jar doon the hill!"

Gregor, Shuggie, and Callum jumped on Stanley, forcing him to the ground, as two burly clansmen grasped the wheel arches of the Mini, toppled it onto its side and off the edge of the road. Stanley could only wriggle and watch as the car bounced and rolled down the grassy slope and off the edge, onto the rocks below. Gregor tied Stanley's hands tightly behind his back and, a few moments later, after being frog-marched up the hill behind them, he looked down the cluster of whitewashed stone and thatched huts that was the McGregor compound.

Finkter knocked twice on the back door.

"Coming," he heard, and then there were footsteps on tiles. Sammy Mellon, landlord of the Black Swan, cracked the door open and peeked out. Finkter could have sworn he heard a stifled laugh, as Mellon closed the door to loosen the chain and then opened it again. He looked over Finkter's shoulder and then from side to side down the alley.

"Did anyone see you coming?" Mellon asked.

"No," Finkter replied. "I came down the back."

Mellon stood aside and motioned for him to come in. Inside, it was dim and smelled of stale beer and rotting carpet. Finkter made his way through the kitchen and into the bar. Virtually no one drank in the Black Swan, or the "Dirty Duck," as it was known, as most of the villagers preferred the atmosphere in the Pig & Spigot, most of which was generated by the caddies. It was the first pub they could stumble into after they got off work and most of them never felt like walking up and over the hill to the next one. Only the occasional visitor to Scroughtly stopped in to the Black Swan, and Mellon, an ex-con and a petty thief, would usually scare them away with his miserable disposition. Today, however, there was a ruddy-faced gentleman with close-cropped gray hair and a huge strawberry nose, wearing a charcoal business suit, seated at the bar when Finkter emerged from the shadows of the kitchen.

The stranger was talking quietly to the obsequious Nigel Oglesby, son of Major Norma Oglesby and a sworn enemy of both his own father, now second mother, and Uncle Dickie since the day on which Reggie Carstairs had nearly killed him. They both sat up and stopped their whispering when Finkter appeared.

"Sergeant, how nice to see you," said Oglesby greasily, getting up and offering Finkter his cold, limp hand.

Finkter was not overjoyed to see Oglesby, who had connections in the village and was known to be a blabbermouth.

"Nigel," he nodded, letting go of the hand as fast as he could.

"Allow me to introduce Sir Stanford Pees, he's one of us."

The ruddy-faced gentleman stood up and offered his much firmer hand to Finkter. Pees had been looking at him rather strangely, and as they shook, he said, "A pleasure I'm sure, but good God, man, what the devil happened to you?"

"A minor altercation last night, when I got ambushed as I went about my duties, but– "

"He got his arse kicked by a man with one leg," Mellon cut in, snorting with laughter as he polished glasses behind the bar.

Finkter whirled around. "Is that who did it?" he barked, pointing a thick finger at him. "It was that old cripple?"

"Never mind, never mind," said Sir Stanford. "We have bigger things to worry about here." He motioned to Finkter, who was breathing heavily and had his teeth clenched. "Sit down, old chap, and listen to what we have to say. I guarantee you, you will have your revenge soon enough."

Finkter sat down and haughtily folded his arms. "All right, you have five minutes," he said. "I have police business to take care of." He was going to find Pogo as soon as he was out of there, he thought: First things first.

Sir Stanford stood up and began to pace around the bar. He motioned to Mellon. "Bring the animals, Mellon, there's a good fellow."

Mellon disappeared into the kitchen and returned carrying a small cage containing two brown furry things. He plunked it down on the table in front of Finkter.

"What do you think those are?" said Sir Stanford, leaning over the table and smiling wickedly.

Finkter peered into the cage. "I don't know, what, like rats or something?"

"No, they're not rats, Sergeant," said Oglesby. "They are a pair of rare and endangered Compton's ferrets, thought to be extinct in the wild here in the British Isles."

Sir Stanford straightened up. "Only they're not," he said. "At least they won't be, when you plant them at the Scrought's Wood Club."

Finkter looked him for a moment, and then at Oglesby, and finally at Mellon. He stared back at the little creatures, which were playing happily in the cage, and for a moment, it felt like his head might explode.

"Why would I do that?"

"Because," began Sir Stanford, as he opened the cage door and pulled one of the ferrets out, "one of them will be dead!" He snapped back the animal's neck and slammed it down on the table, where it lay twitching.

Finkter's eyes almost popped out of his head. "Bloody hell!" he gasped. "What'd you do that for?"

Sir Stanford sat down at the table and began to stroke the lifeless little body. "Finkter, I did it because you would like to see these people out of your town; Oglesby would like to see their club closed down; and Mellon would like some customers."

"What's in it for you?" asked Mellon.

"Etiquette, honor, and decency. I'm doing it in the name of all that is right in this world and for my Queen!" replied Stanford.

At the mention of the Queen, Finkter melted. Stanford stood

up holding the animal by its tail. "Now, I want you to take these animals," he said, returning the dead ferret to its cage, "and release the live one. Then I want you to toss the dead one to the dog I've been hearing about, Digby, or whatever his name is, and take a photo of him sniffing, chewing, or whatever he does to it. When the National Trust, or the WWF, or whomever catches wind of the fact that this animal is back in these parts, and in grave danger, we will have succeeded. Every left-handed, liberal, vegetarian, lesbian, whale-humping, shrub-hugging, bomb-banning cretin in the universe will be howling for the immediate closure of the club!"

Sir Stanford's oratory and his aristocratic bearing mesmerized Finkter, whose jaw had dropped open. Finally, he thought, Here was a chance to do something exciting in this festering dung heap of a village. The WWF reference had confused him for a second, but hey, if those wrestling people wanted to get upset about this as well, that was just fine by him. He had heard the Queen Mother was a fan.

Sir Stanford hadn't finished. He stood up and pointed at Oglesby. "What else will they be howling for, Oglesby?" he asked quietly.

Oglesby was caught off guard. "Well, I…er, I'm not sure, Stanford old boy," he said. "But I have a feeling you're going to tell me."

Sir Stanford turned to face Finkter, and put his hand on his shoulder. "No," he said. "I'm going to tell Sergeant Finkter. Because they will be howling for the ARREST, FINKTER!" he shouted, "and the IMMEDIATE INCARCERATION! of anyone who might be involved in the loss of one of the last remaining examples of this beautiful creature." He pointed at the cage, pulled out a linen handkerchief from the breast pocket of his jacket, steadied himself with a hand on the edge of the table, and dabbed at his eyes in mock grief.

Finkter now had an erection and was gazing at Sir Stanford with an expression of enraptured adoration.

"Incarceration?" he said as tears of joy welled up in his eyes. "You mean we can actually set fire to them?"

Sir Stanford stared at Finkter blankly for a moment and then said, "Absolutely."

CHAPTER NINE

Hamish appeared to be in a hypnotic trance, his face dripping with sweat as he danced around the bonfire to the reel that blared on the boom box. He held the digit in its wooden box above his head as the rest of the clan whooped and cheered wildly. Occasionally he stopped to pull one of his men out to the fire's edge to throw a shot of the McGregor malt into the blaze, which fired the celebration to new heights. Shuggie had made sure that there was no power problem this time and had the boom box plugged into an outlet in his hut by way of a long extension cord.

Inside the hut, listening to the pagan gloating, Stanley stood, tied to the cast-iron chimney of a potbellied stove. Occasionally, Shuggie, who was enjoying the opportunity to be the tormentor for a change, would visit him for a wee private gloat. The stove, which had been a little too hot for Stanley's comfort at first, had now cooled a little, although his legs were aching and he longed for the opportunity to sit down. The door banged open, and Shuggie came in to see how he was doing.

"Ooh, hullo," he leered, his chubby face floating in front of Stanley's. "How's the temperature, ye one-nut wonder? Ah hope that wee raisin of yours is no' goin' tae freeze on us now, so maybe ah'd better throw a couple of logs intae the stove, what d'ye think?"

Stanley watched as Shuggie lurched over to the stove, and tossed in some firewood, followed by the contents of his glass, a full half-pint of single malt. The fire inside roared into life as he clanged the door shut.

"Och aye, tha's much more like it, isn't it?" Shuggie said mockingly. "Toodle-pip now, old boy, ah'll see ye a wee bit later!"

Stanley remained silent as the fat clansman left, and braced himself as the heat grew more intense. If he could only break free he thought, the clan were so preoccupied with their celebration, perhaps he could make his escape unnoticed. Despite his discomfort as the fire grew hotter and hotter, what really worried him was the fact that he had let Uncle Dickie down. This was more than he could bear, and as the heat from the chimney started to blister the back of his forearms, the tears that ran down his face and onto his lips were more from shame than from pain.

It was not the first time that Stanley had been brave, or stupid either. He cursed himself and pulled as hard as he could on the nylon rope that bound his wrists. The cord cut into his flesh, making him shudder as he strained forward, and the back of his trousers started to smolder as he backed into the pipe for leverage. It was then that he noticed that the heat was not only melting him, but the nylon cord, too.

None of the McGregors heard the scream as Stanley gave his all in a huge, final, agonizing tug. The cord melted and gave way, hardening into a thin, stiff wisp, and Stanley fell sobbing to the mud floor. He lay silently for a moment, then gathered himself, crept to the door, and eased it open. The light from the bonfire flickered wildly across his eyes as he watched Hamish twirl insanely across the mud, one arm around the ancient wooden box and the other flailing wildly skyward. At this point in the proceedings, it was obvious there was no way he could sneak out of the hut without being noticed, so Stanley made his way over to the other side of the room, slid himself under Shuggie McGregor's bed, and waited.

The bed had looked relatively flat on top to Stanley, but the enormous downward pressure that Shuggie had exerted upon it for years had destroyed the springs below, which were almost on the ground. Stanley knew as soon as he got under there, that he wasn't going to be able to stand it for long. He could barely squeeze into the narrow space, which was littered with foil wrappers from slabs of chocolate, and Styrofoam fast-food containers, which had attracted a variety of insects to the scene. He did his best to keep still, but when something started to feed on his already blistered and bleeding forearms, Stanley realized that this latest idea of his was up to his normal standards.

Fortunately, it didn't take long for the dung to hit the windmill. Shuggie, by now hopelessly drunk, made another courtesy call on his captive, and he sobered up considerably when he found that Stanley was missing. Stanley knew that the chase was on when, from under the bed, he watched Shuggie blunder over to the wall, and pull out the power cord to the boom box, which put a swift end to the revelry outside. Moments later, Hamish stumbled in, followed by Callum and Jockie.

Hamish was bulletproof drunk and had one foot nailed to the floor, as he moved the other one around to keep his balance. It took a while for it to register that Stanley was missing. As Stanley held his breath under the bed, a large beetle crawled up and over his face. He closed his mouth and eyes as tightly as he could.

Across the room, Hamish was staring at the hapless figure of Shuggie, who stood and twiddled his thumbs nervously.

"What'd ye do, Shuggie?" he said drunkenly, taking a couple of unsteady steps closer to him. Shuggie was speechless and looked terrified.

"Ye fuckin' ate him, didn't ye, ye fat sack of crap," Hamish spat.

"No, Hamish, ah didnae," bleated Shuggie.

Hamish whirled around, glared at Callum and Jockie, and yelled, "Don't just stand there then, go an' find the bastard!" Then he fell over backward with a thump, his long, bony fingers still wrapped around the box.

Shuggie peered down at him, and then back at Callum and Jockie.

"Looks like he's oot," he said with a sigh of relief.

Callum turned and headed for the door. "Come on, Jockie," he said. "Let's go and gettim'. He had tae head back over the hill or we wud've seen him."

"Bollocks," muttered Shuggie, and lumbered after them.

Stanley wriggled out from under the bed and shuddered as he wiped himself down. He felt like screaming. Hamish lay flat out on the earthen floor, with the box on his chest, covered by his left arm. He was snoring loudly as Stanley tiptoed over, past where he lay, and over to the open doorway. Stanley was about to slip out and make his way across the deserted compound, when something stopped him. He turned and looked at the prostrate figure of the McGregor Chieftain. Here was a chance, he thought, to redeem himself and to make everything right. Quivering with fear, Stanley Beamish crept back and bent over Hamish. Taking a huge breath, he gently picked up the thin forearm of the snoring clansman with one hand and, with his other hand, lifted the box. Trembling, he gently lowered Hamish's arm back to his chest, tucked the box under his arm, and crept silently back to the door. Suddenly, Hamish inhaled noisily, and held his breath. Stanley froze and waited for the inevitable, but to his relief, the only sounds that followed were of a long wet, involuntary fart, followed by the smacking of lips and then regular, deep breathing. As Stanley slipped out and into the darkness, he saw the flicker of flashlights crisscrossing the hill in front of him. He slithered around the side of the hut and, through the flickering shadows of the dying campfire, headed for the beach.

There was just enough moonlight to give a ghostly shimmer to the estuary as he picked his way among the rocks and seaweed. Stanley clutched his prize tightly under his arm and shivered violently, his breath crystallizing back into his face as he walked along the shore. He knew if he kept the water to his left, he was heading back toward Carnoustie, where he could telephone Uncle Dickie.

Twenty minutes later, he came across an unexpected bonus. The Mini had come to rest well above the waterline and was resting on its wheels. All the windows were smashed and it was badly dented all over, but his bag was still inside and the keys were still in the ignition. He grabbed his stuff, pocketed the keys, and after a quick stop to bathe his blisters in the brine, set off down the beach.

Uncle Dickie sat at his desk, drumming his fingers and staring at the Maharajah.

"Where the hell do you suppose he is?" he said, looking anxiously at his wristwatch.

The Maharajah closed the book he had been examining and took a sip of his tea. "If there is one thing about Beamish that we can be sure of, Dickie," he said, "it would be that he has most definitely landed with his arse in the flames. Surely you know that, my old friend. To be honest with you, I have never been able to understand why you would put any faith in him at all. I know you are fond of him and that he is loyal, brave, and trustworthy, but he has the IQ of a pickled egg."

Uncle Dickie let out a sigh. "Yes, I know, Poony, but he deserves a chance to get it right once. It would make such a difference to his life, to the way he regards himself, if he could triumph over an adversary, without help from anyone else or from me. I can imagine the look on his face and I want to see it."

The Maharajah drew a deep breath and shook his head. "I do not know of anyone like you, Dickie. In all the years that we have been friends, I have never seen you put your own ambitions or desires before these people, none of whom could possibly make a difference in your life. Have you ever done so?"

"Well," began Uncle Dickie, "you see, Poony, things are not always as they seem, I mean– "

But just then the telephone on Uncle Dickie's desk jangled into life. "Excuse me, old boy," he said, and picked up the handset.

Stanley was in a public phone box at a bus stop on the outskirts of Carnoustie. He was shaking with cold, and his legs were soaked to the knee from wading through the icy shallows along the shoreline.

"Major General, sir, it's me, Beamish," he said excitedly.

Uncle Dickie stood up. "Beamish!" he exclaimed, "Where the devil are you, and what have you been doing?"

"Don't worry, sir, I have the most wonderful news," Stanley said, doing his best to stop his teeth from chattering. "I have the digit with me, sir, I rescued it from the McGregors."

"You did what?" said Uncle Dickie, incredulous. "Beamish, you idiot, I ordered you to go up there and scout out the lay of the land. You had no business going in there and taking the Digit. Put it back immediately!"

Stanley couldn't believe his ears. "I-I-I beg your pardon, sir?" he said, "I'm not sure that I heard you correctly. Did you say, 'Put it back?'"

Uncle Dickie covered the mouthpiece and looked at the Maharajah, who was wearing an I-told-you-so expression. "Yes," he said quietly. "I said put it back, and make sure they don't know it was gone. I'll be up there shortly. Have you got that?"

"Yes, sir," said Stanley. "Right away, sir," and hung up.

Uncle Dickie replaced the receiver, and said to the Maharajah, "As I was saying, things are not always as they seem."

"And as I was saying," said the Maharajah. "Beamish is an

idiot."

Uncle Dickie frowned, "How the devil will I know how to play that course now, Poony?"

Poony shrugged and sipped his tea.

Stanley was dumbfounded once more. He stumbled out of the phone box, and absentmindedly stuck out his thumb as a Land Rover pulling a horse trailer, driven by a small gnarly old man, rumbled by. It came to a stop about fifty yards down the road.

Stanley shambled down the road and stopped outside the passenger window, as the man rolled it down.

"Where ye goin'?" the old man said.

"To the McGregor homestead," Stanley blurted out.

"Ooh, ah see," said the old man looking a little puzzled. "A friend of theirs, are ye?"

"Not exactly," said Stanley. "In fact, quite the opposite."

The man looked at Stanley and laughed. "Aye, that makes ye and the rest of the English-speaking world. Ye don't have tae tell me, ah own the land tae the east of them, an' they're a menace tae me. Hop in."

Stanley climbed up into the vehicle, and the old man set off. Stanley clung to the wooden box like a suicide bomber, for that was exactly how he was feeling. Nevertheless, he put his seat belt on.

"Wha's in the box?" the old man asked.

"The petrified middle finger of St. Andrew," Stanley said, as he gazed vacantly out the window at the firth.

The old man looked at Stanley as if he had a dead rabbit

hanging out of his nose. "Is tha' a fact?" he said. "What're ye goin' tae dae with that?"

Stanley looked at him. There wasn't a lot of point at this stage, he felt, in trying to make up any kind of a story, as the truth seemed quite unbelievable enough. "I, sir," he announced, "Am going to sneak into the McGregor camp, and plant this box for them to find it, and then I am going to make my escape, without them noticing."

"An how dae ye think yer goin' tae do that?"

"I have absolutely no idea."

The old man drove on in silence for a while, until Stanley noticed the Mini down on the shore. "Thanks a lot," he said. "This'll do me here."

But the old man drove on. "No, really," Stanley said, "I have to get out here, thank you."

The old man took his right hand off the wheel and reached over. "Forgive me," he said. "I didnae introduce mahself. McGregor's the name. Hamilton McGregor, but ma friends call me Hammy."

Stanley had already grasped his callused hand before the horror set in. The old man saw the look on his face and said, "Och, nivver worry, son, ah'm the black sheep o' the family. Tha' means you can call me Hammy, too." He threw his head back and laughed. "Let's see if we can't get that wee box of yours back where it belongs!"

Stanley smiled. "Beamish," he said. "Stanley Beamish. Nice to meet you, Hammy."

CHAPTER TEN

U ncle Dickie stood at the conservatory window and stared disconcertedly out into the garden. Beating Hamish McGregor in his own backyard would be difficult enough, but with no knowledge of the golf course, he knew it was going be well nigh impossible. Auntie Myrtle's head appeared from behind a row of rose bushes. She waved and blew him a kiss, as he tapped on the window and motioned to her to come inside. She set her pruning shears down and wiped her hands on her apron, making her way up the narrow stone path to the steps, where Uncle Dickie opened the door and, taking her hand, ushered her in.

"Sorry to bother you, old girl," he said. "But I need another spot of advice."

Auntie Myrtle smiled gently and sat down. "I see," she said, straightening her apron. "Battle plans again?"

"Precisely," Uncle Dickie grumbled. "Or the lack thereof." He sat down heavily in the wicker chair opposite, and rubbed his temples. "Beamish has failed to reconnoiter the Tay Club, and now the McGregors are expecting us. I simply have to get a look at the course before I take on Hamish, but now we've been rumbled."

Auntie Myrtle shook her head sympathetically and folded her arms. "Why don't you catch up on some reading in the dungeon while I give it a bit of thought."

"Ooh, what a dashed good idea that is!" Uncle Dickie said energetically. "The Tomes!" He sprang out of the chair and marched up the steps into the library, where he pulled out a grubby first edition score of Handel's *Messiah*. Aunt Myrtle watched him, smiling and shaking her head. Silently, the wall of books swung open, revealing a damp stone stairwell leading down into the darkness. He opened the book, took out a concealed flashlight, and made his way carefully down the stairs, pulling the wall of books closed behind him. Grasping a pig-iron handle, he pulled open the heavy oak door to the dungeon and groped around on the wall just inside the vaulted doorway. When he flipped on the light switch, he heard the yowl of a cat. A grayish blur shot across the flagstones in front of him, followed by Poultice, the fat tortoiseshell, who skidded to a clumsy halt as his furry quarry wriggled into a crack in the wall and disappeared. Poultice stuck a paw into the hole after the mouse, and then turned to arch his back and hiss viciously at Uncle Dickie. Uncle Dickie's brow furrowed as he stood with his hands on his hips.

"Hmmm," he said sternly. "Don't blame me Poultice, you fat fur ball. If you'd spend a little less time in the kitchen, and a little more in the garden, you might develop some hunting skills. Go on, get out!"

He shooed the angry cat out the door with his foot, closed the door, and made his way over to what looked like a large humidor.

Deep underneath the limestone floors of Gussett Hall, the dungeon had for centuries lain in damp and darkness, until Uncle Dickie had it refurbished into a secret den, into which he occasionally retired to read in private. Inside the glass-fronted cabinet in a carefully controlled atmosphere, bound in gold-leaf and leather-spined volumes, lay the precious records of his family's history, the ancient records of Gussett Hall, and Brother Dick's original layout maps of Scrought's Wood golf course. He reached up to one of the top shelves and pulled out one of the most decrepit-looking manuscripts.

"Ah, yes," he muttered to himself as he undid the gold clasp, and the book creaked open where he placed it, on a magnificent walnut Chippendale desk. "The matches of 1650. The holy war." Uncle Dickie sat down to read.

Throughout its checkered and often ghastly history, the walls of Gussett Hall had provided sanctuary for a wide variety of saints and scoundrels. The seventeenth century was of particular interest to Uncle Dickie, as in the spring of 1650, the first match had taken place between the members of the Wood and the McGregors. At the time, Oliver Cromwell had overthrown the reigning Stuarts and declared England a republic, and his men were scouring the countryside, searching for and often torturing and executing Roman Catholic priests, just for the hell of it. While Cromwell and his Ironsides were off laying waste to Ireland, the Lord of Gussett Hall, none other than Cardinal Egbert Gussett, had decided to take up temporary residence north of the border in Scotland, where the Royalists were still in charge, and had built himself a home away from home in the old gray town of St. Andrews. It wasn't long before he felt the urge to play a little golf, but due to his abrasive personality and outspoken derision for their rules, he was blackballed by the small band of golfers at St. Andrews, and was forced to find an alternative venue to exercise his passion. He had heard of a band of wild and woolly clansmen who claimed to have invented a similar game on a tract of land along the Firth of Tay, so he and his small flock of monks packed up and headed for Dundee, and the lair of the McGregors.

Cardinal Egbert Gussett, for whom the local infirmary in Scroughtly was named, presided over a small enclave of monks who were renowned throughout the country for their medical expertise and ran a very profitable clinic that pandered to some of the common ailments afflicting the wealthy folk of the time. Uncle Dickie pored over the beautifully embellished script, with its descriptions of how to treat "Crotchpox, Weevil Eye, and the Dreaded Lurgy." He turned the yellowing pages until he found what he was looking for.

The Cardinal had been no less keen a golfer than any other keeper of Gussett Hall. He had kept faithful records of both the development of Scrought's Wood and their relationship with the rival Tay Club north of the border. Before Uncle Dickie lay the first known map of the McGregors' three-hole golf course. He stroked his chin thoughtfully as he studied the Cardinal's work. Every hazard was marked and named, with changes in elevation and comments about how the course should be tackled. Cardinal Egbert had plotted the position where each of his shots had landed during the famous first match between himself and the evil Hugh McGregor, a man as famous for his cruelty as he was for the legendary size of his genitals. According to McGregor lore, there was no sporran big enough for Hugh "Huge" McGregor.

Tracing a manicured finger across the parchment, Uncle

Dickie noticed a vast, featureless area known as the "Desperation Flats," in the middle of the second hole, which also had what appeared to be a deep cleft in the fairway just short of the green. The cleft sloped steeply downward to the shore and a rock formation known as "The Nostril," beside which the Cardinal had inscribed a note: "Venture not."

"Hmmm," mumbled Uncle Dickie, "I'll take the old boy's word on that one." On the next page, the Cardinal had written a full account of the events of the match that had started the rivalry between the two clubs. Uncle Dickie slipped a pair of half-moon reading glasses out of his breast pocket, pulled a bottle of Louis XIII cognac from his desk drawer, and poured himself a massive snifter. Then he settled himself in his chair and began to read about the historic morning upon which Huge McGregor had awakened to find a tall, imposing Roman Catholic clergyman dressed in full-length, ermine-trimmed red velvet and a great big pointy red helmet, banging the bejesus out of his front door with a ruby-and-diamond-encrusted crozier.

It was an hour before noon, when the heathen saw fit to emerge from his squalid den, and join me upon the teeing ground, which, like the rest of the foul pasture these savages call their "Links," was festooned with the turds of sheep. Still, with his arrival, the already present stench did greatly increase. Much had I heard from his kinfolk, of the mighty size of his manhood, and indeed, as he swung his heavy driving wassock from side to side in preparation for the game, the magnitude of his unmentionables was clearly evident beneath the folds of his pagan vestments. Lest I had any doubt, before he took his first cut, he did raise the skirts of his dress, and proclaim loudly, that after the game he did intend to insert the vile organ into my holy personage, a claim so unseemly, that my holy quill does refuse to inscribe it herein. Verily, let it be sufficient to say, that all the holy water in Christendom would not have purified the mouth of such a godless, boorish, ill-bred son of a syphilitic cloven-footed goat buggerer. Forgive me, dear Lord, for I know not what I write.

"Dearie me!" exclaimed Uncle Dickie, pushing his half-moon reading glasses up his nose. He took another sip, and read on.

But I digress. In order to assure that the resounding beating I would deal to McGregor would indeed be certified as valid, and thus assure the digit should rest for evermore in the Wood of the Eternal Scrought, I had taken the precaution of requesting the presence of independent counsel, in the form of a referee. The umpire of the game, McCracken, was a fancy fellow indeed, from the Honorable Company of Edinburgh Golfers, a band of red-coated bourgeois upstarts, who seem to consider themselves in some way expert in the laws of the game. But no sooner than McCracken started to announce his rules upon the teeing ground, he, all in white stockings and buttons of gold, the horrible McGregor dealt the unfortunate man a terrible blow to his pate with a spring-faced todger, sending his powdered wig asunder, and rendering him lacking in sense for not an inconsiderable time. Such a savage and painful event I had not witnessed, since Brother Percy the Pansy was radished by Cuthbert the gardener before the harvest festival last autumn.

Uncle Dickie screwed up his eyes, took a sip of his brandy, and read the passage again. "*Radished*? Surely that should read *ravished*." He looked closer.

"Nope," he shrugged, "that definitely says *radished*." He read on.

Nevertheless, the savage and I agreed to play under the originals, and before long, the true nature of his character was revealed. He is a man of great strength, this McGregor, but as I had expected, his skills are limited to the heavier bludgeons alone. Once around the sacred pit, his courage deserted him, and he was reduced to a timorous shivering wreck. On the first hole, he was on the grass of great shortness in four cuts less than my divine self, but so great was the frequency of his nudging, I found myself with the advantage as we began the second hole.

Great was McGregor's anger with his kinfolk, many of whom scattered ahead, as we traversed the Flats of Desperation. Many unseen hazards did I visit there, and for the better part of the second hole, the foe did disappear from my view. Unknown to me was the Nostril that lies before the second grass of great shortness, and great misfortune did it bring. Woe betide the unwary in its presence, let ye be warned.

Uncle Dickie sat back in his chair, took a long sip of his brandy, and let out a long, thoughtful breath. "I'm going to have to investigate this place thoroughly," he said to himself, pushing his spectacles back up his nose and leaning over the manuscript once more.

The third and final hole is the most arduous on the McGregors' land, and if not for the grace of the heavenly father, one that I surely would have lost. The steams of the sea did envelop us, and upon the teeing ground it seemed as if the sky had fallen. It was a practice cut with my driving crozier I did make, that sent the McGregor Chieftain off the edge of the abyss. So thick was the mist, I did not see him, and at first I thought I had walloped one of the many faithful sheep that did follow him, but a flash of tartan cloth and his pendulous dangling wobblers I glimpsed, as I, by the purest of chance, did hit him one time more on my follow through. Then, as fate would have it, as I bludgeoned my tee shot in earnest, his ugly countenance did appear like a wraith once more in front of me. He had clambered up the cliff, and his nose did hit my speeding feathery a fearsome crack, causing me to lose my best feathery bollock. No, honest, I did. But hell had one more to burn, and t'was the will of God, no doubt.

Uncle Dickie raised his eyebrows. "Hmm, no doubt indeed," he said as he closed the book and returned it to the shelf above. He pulled down a second volume, and began to flick through it. After the suspicious goings-on of the first match, the McGregor clan had engaged in frequent correspondence with the various masters of Gussett Hall. Throughout the ages, the letters gradually became more and more adversarial in nature, and as Uncle Dickie refreshed his memory of the history between the two sides, it became ever more obvious to him that a visit to the Tay Club was essential, if he were to be faithful to the memory of his ancestors. Back and forth, the insults had been flung, with one match every fifty years, and as Uncle Dickie read on, it occurred to him that he was looking at snapshots of the game's evolution, alongside the development of one of the greatest rivalries in the history of sport. The ancient parchments were filled with descriptions of the three-hole course, which, as Uncle Dickie had suspected, had not been altered in any way since the game was born. In some of the more recent manuscripts, there were even some grainy black-and-white photographs of grim-faced clansmen and members before battle had begun. Uncle Dickie recognized the face of Sir Basil Strangely-Smallpiece, staring at him from a photograph that had presumably been taken just a few hours before his untimely demise.

The one thing that was missing from his family's history was a Gussett who had won on both battlegrounds. He had just won the digit fair and square on his own territory, but a win on the McGregors' soil would be so much sweeter. Now that the digit had been stolen, he had what he wanted: a legitimate reason to go and challenge the McGregor Chieftain in his own back yard.

He looked around the dimly lit room, with its portraits of the ancient Gussetts and strange-looking golf artifacts on the wall. The eyes of each of his forebears seemed to be smiling at him, willing him on, and this filled him with a sense of righteous indignation. He stood up, pulled down his tweed waistcoat, jutted out his chin, and grabbed an ancient-looking hickory-shafted club from its mount on the wall.

"Ahh," he gasped with glee. "An original Bungley backup wedge!"

He addressed an imaginary ball on the stone floor, and gave the club a couple of waggles.

"You shall come with me, my beauty, for your golfing days are not done just yet!"

And with that, he tucked the club underneath his arm, returned the book to the shelf, tossed back the brandy, and turned out the light. A spring in his step, he made his way back upstairs to the library and began pacing anxiously on the black-and-white marble floor, while plotting strategy, his hands tightly clasped behind his back.

"I do wish you'd sit down, darling," Auntie Myrtle said from her wicker chair in the adjoining conservatory. Outside, the sun was setting, and the last sliver of orange fire had dipped below the great wall that flanked the fourth hole.

Uncle Dickie turned, and looked in the bay window at the reflection of his wife of fifty-two years, as she gazed out at the perfect little courtyard garden, in which she spent most of her time. How he loved her, he thought.

They had met in an army hospital in Rangoon, where he was recovering from a stomach wound he had received in a land mine explosion in Burma. He had been leading a detachment of men down a jungle road, as always, from the front, when he heard the roar and felt the searing pain. Hers was the first face he saw when he regained consciousness, and he remembered the moment as if it were yesterday. She was a vision of incomparable loveliness, with long shining raven hair that tumbled from her face and over her shoulders. Uncle Dickie thought then, as he did now, that he might have died and gone to heaven. For weeks, she had tended his wounds, bathed his body, and nurtured his spirit. As he stood there gazing at her reflection, he felt an uplifting rush of adrenaline as he thought of the moment, some months later, when she had agreed without hesitation to marry him. The hair on his neck bristled, he shivered, and felt gooseflesh on his forearms as the courtyard floodlights snapped on, and suddenly her reflection in the window was gone. He straightened and walked softly into the conservatory, where he took Auntie Myrtle by the hand. She rose, and pulled out his shirttail, slipping a slender arm around his waist, and gently ran her fingertips along the wicked scar on his belly. The skin was looser than it used to be, but underneath, Uncle Dickie's muscle was still firm to the touch.

He smiled, and looked down into her shining brown eyes.

"You always know the answer, don't you, my love?"

"I've always known the answer to you," she said.

"Did I tell you today that I love you?"

"Only about a dozen times, which isn't enough." Auntie Myrtle smiled. She sat down again and looked out the window. "You have to leave, I suppose."

Uncle Dickie looked at the floor, and rocked back and forth on his heels. "Yes my dear, I do."

"My gallant soldier is rushing into battle one last time, is that it?"

"Probably," he said. "But I have the evening to spend with my love." He placed a foot on either side of the wicker chair, and cradled his wife in his arms. He lifted and carried her to the two steps up to the library, where he faltered a little as he ascended.

Auntie Myrtle had her arms around his neck, her eyes locked

on his.

"Careful," she teased, as he gathered himself, and made for the bedroom door. "You're not as young as you used to be."

"We'll see about that," he said, back-heeling the door closed behind him.

CHAPTER ELEVEN

Flanagan struggled under the weight of the two golf bags, each of which held about thirty clubs. Oversize drivers, strange looking irons, and various putters of differing lengths sprouted from Uncle Dickie's auxiliary bag, while the main bag, which he used for everyday play, carried two sets of Ben Hogan irons, a couple of shallow-faced fairway woods, and an old Cash-In putter. Uncle Dickie's irons are separated by only two degrees of loft, rather than the usual four, which would explain the two sets to most people, except of course for the man who has to carry his bags. Around Scrought's Wood, the game is played with whatever equipment is necessary, but on this particular morning, as Flanagan heaved the bags into the back of the caddie wagon, he was wishing that the Rules of Golf applied.

The previous evening had provided Flanagan with little sleep, as Dwilby, who was rapidly becoming his nemesis, had gotten the better of him once more. Dwilby had been rooting in the discarded leftovers behind the kitchen and had just eaten, then coughed up, a mound of rancid tripe and onions, when Agnes let him in for the evening. As usual, as Flanagan lay sleeping with his wife, Dwilby had jumped onto the foot of the bed, and snuggled against Agnes's back, but on this occasion, just before he had nodded off, he had slipped out a tiny, but mind-bendingly pungent fart. A few moments later, Agnes had awakened with a yell, and beaten Flanagan out of the bed and onto the sofa in the other room.

Flanagan had been in a dead enough sleep at the time to believe that he was the guilty party, but after he had spent a few minutes on the sofa, he let out a fart of his own devices, and instantly noticed a difference in the aroma. His was as aromatic as a freshly baked loaf of bread by comparison, he thought, and in fact, it was really quite nice. He spent the rest of the night tossing, turning, and silently cursing the dog.

Thirsty stood at the back of the caddie wagon, and drained a bottle of Guinness as the last of the clubs were loaded. He let out a loud, guttural burp and wiped his mouth on his sleeve.

"Where's all the good stuff?" he asked Flanagan, who was rubbing his temples as if he was in pain.

"The old man'll be takin' those in the Bentley, there's no way he'd let them out of his sight," said Flanagan. "Ah've heard the bangstick is goin' too."

"Bugger me!" said Thirsty. "He must be deadly serious."

Uncle Dickie's ancient golf club collection contains some of the rarest and finest implements in the world, many of which are the only examples of their kind, and worth hundreds of thousands, if not millions of dollars in today's market. That any of them would actually be used for play was beyond conception for even Thirsty, unless of course there was alcohol involved in the bet, in which case, all bets were off, which would make no sense to anyone, except Thirsty.

Thirsty McManus had been over the legal limit for driving when awake for as long as he could remember, and that was the way everyone liked to keep him. He almost never ate, and almost never stopped drinking. Thirsty stood only five feet, two inches tall, and was skinny as a whip. Uncle Dickie said that when Thirsty was sober, he was the most violent human being over whom he'd ever held command. Once, in Burma, after losing his weapon, Thirsty found himself cut off from the rest of his battalion, and Uncle Dickie dispatched a group of Ghurkas to rescue him. Some hours later, they were astonished to find him sitting on a tree stump, surrounded by several dead and dying enemy men, drinking a bottle of gin.

"I smelt it," he had apparently said.

He looked at Flanagan and said remorsefully, "I wish I wuz goin', Seamus. I really do."

Flanagan sat down heavily on the bench outside the caddie-shack, and looked at him, grinning.

"You are goin', Thirsty. An' so is Tweezer, an' Mills, an' Boon!"

Thirsty's face lit up. He dropped the empty bottle and thrust two small, knotted fists in the air.

"Yes!" he shouted. "You wee beauty, Seamus!" and started to dance a jig around the van.

"There's just one thing, wee man," Seamus said, his face suddenly grave. "Uncle Dickie wants ye to be sober tomorrow. There could be fisticuffs."

"If I'm sober, there most certainly will be."

"Come on," said Flanagan. "Help me load the rest of the stuff into the van. The old man'll be here any minute."

Flanagan heard the crunching of tires on gravel behind him

as he and Thirsty were loading the last of the equipment and provisions into the caddie wagon. Uncle Dickie drew up alongside them in a brand-new white Bedford panel van, and hopped out of the driver's seat nimbly.

"Good morning, Flanagan," he said breezily, clapping his hands together and rubbing them vigorously together. "A chill in the air, the sun in the sky, a fresh breeze, and a road trip! What could be better?" Flanagan had not seen the old man in such a mood for quite a while. Uncle Dickie laughed and turned to Thirsty.

"Thirsty, go and find Tweezer, there's a good fellow, and tell him his Uncle Dickie has a surprise for him."

Thirsty snapped his heels together and saluted smartly. "Sir, yes, sir!" he shouted, spun on his heel, and disappeared quickly into the caddieshack.

Uncle Dickie opened the driver's side door, and flipped back a couple of levers under the seat.

"Come have a look at this, Flanagan, " he said, as he leaned against the seat, and shoved it sideways into the center of the vehicle. Flanagan looked on curiously, as Thirsty reappeared, pushing Tweezer up the ramp from the caddieshack.

"Ah, Tweezer my boy," Uncle Dickie said, smiling broadly, and slamming the driver's door. "I thought it was about time we got you a bit more mobile. Come with me around the back."

"Yes, sir," said Tweezer, pushing himself alongside the van, and looking up at its high sides. Uncle Dickie flung open one of the back doors and reached inside to push a button, and an electric motor whirred, as a wheelchair lift slowly descended to the ground. Tweezer looked on with boyish excitement, and asked Uncle Dickie, "Sir, can I, I mean... am I going to be allowed to drive it?"

Uncle Dickie hunkered down beside him, and looked in his eyes, which were rapidly filling with tears. Danny Bickerstaff, aka "Tweezer," was so named because of his skills in the area of bomb disposal. Before his accident, which had left him paralyzed from the waist down, he had been part of the legendary "Felix" unit on active service in Northern Ireland. A tiny nail bomb, hidden underneath the one he had just successfully defused, had changed his life forever. It was just an ounce of C4, and a dozen six-inch nails, one of which had found its way through the gaps in the Kevlar, and his spinal cord. Even though he had never served under Uncle Dickie, Seamus Flanagan, in the old man's Bentley, had picked him up the day he was discharged from hospital. He was brought to the Scrought's Wood club, where he had met Major General Sir Richard Gussett (retired), for the first time.

Uncle Dickie had been told that the boy, who was only twenty-two years old at the time, was deeply depressed and had, during his hospitalization, attempted to take his own life several times.

Instead, Uncle Dickie had taken his life, and given it back to him. Today was just another step, for a man who could no longer walk.

"My boy," Uncle Dickie said, "You can do whatever you like in it, it's yours. There is only one condition upon which I shall insist you agree. I want you to continue to push yourself up to the Pig & Spigot every day, at least once." He grabbed the disabled man by his powerful upper arms and squeezed them hard. "You are strong and hard, and you have fought to be like this. Don't give it away!"

Tweezer looked at him and pulled himself together.

"You have my word, sir!"

"Excellent!" said Uncle Dickie. "Now, just push yourself onto the platform, lock the brake, and push the button."

A few moments later, Tweezer had rolled himself behind the wheel, and wound down the window.

"Throttle and brake under your right thumb, clutch under your left," said Uncle Dickie. "Push down to change down, and up to change up. Couldn't be simpler."

Tweezer looked down from the window at Uncle Dickie. "Thank you so much, sir, I can't tell you how much I—"

"I know, my boy, I know. But it's nothing less than you deserve," he said. "Now go on, take her for a spin!"

Tweezer drew a deep breath and turned the key. He settled himself in his chair, pushed down with both thumbs, and the van took off with a couple of kangaroo hops toward the entrance to the club. A clenched fist appeared from the driver's window, and Flanagan, Thirsty, and Uncle Dickie heard a whoop of joy, as the vehicle disappeared between the hedges of Hadrian's Lane.

"Well, then, boys," Uncle Dickie said energetically. "Let's talk battle plans. Flanagan, if you would be so kind, find Mills and Boon, and meet me in my office in five minutes."

Agnes sat on the step outside the cottage, and tossed a corner from her ham sandwich to Dwilby, who caught it neatly, and chugged it down like a seagull. He sat down and looked at her imploringly, wagging his tail, which Agnes had refused to have docked. He lifted a paw. "Oooh," Agnes cooed, reaching down and scratching his back. "You're such a good wee fella, y'know that, don't ye?"

Dwilby did know that, and he also knew that there was some kind of a new female in town that needed a large portion of his kind of loving. He had caught a whiff of something in heat on the breeze this morning. As soon as he had exhausted the possibility that he might get more of this sandwich, that was where he was headed.

Agnes tossed him her last bite, and kissed him on the nose as he ate it. She got up and went inside to get another basket of clothes to peg on the line, and Dwilby headed for the big smoke of Scroughtly pausing only for a quick squirt on the gatepost on the way out of the club.

Finkter was grinning like a grand piano as he sidled in through the back door to the police station, holding the large cardboard box. He started to hum to himself, as he swiped his car keys off the desk, and broke into song, as he flung open the front door and stepped out.

"Ole, ole, ole, ole," he yelled tunelessly, as he held the box in one hand, and fumbled to open the door to his battered little Yugo. This, and, "God save the Queen," were the only songs to which he knew the lyrics. As he carefully placed the box on the backseat, an elderly lady walked by. Quickly, he unfolded his gangling body from the interior of the car.

"Hello, Mrs. Crump!" he said gaily. "How are the hemorrhoids today? Not too irritating, I hope?"

Mrs. Crump looked at him and recoiled, obviously shocked by his mutilated appearance, and backed away down the pavement.

Undaunted, Finkter shouted: "Splendid!" and settled himself behind the wheel. He slammed the door, and considered for a moment whether or not he should use his flashing lights and siren, but decided against it. As much as he would love to, this was not the time. Better to keep undercover, and leave the bells and whistles for the arrest and incarceration bit at the end. He clapped his hands together, turned the key, and the car coughed to life.

Finkter drove to the bottom of the street where the road got narrow, and was just about to burst into song once more, when suddenly, a big white van came careering around the corner in front of him. Finkter held ground on his side of the road, but as the van got closer it became evident that the driver was paying absolutely no attention to the road in front.

"BLOODY HELL!" Finkter screamed, as he yanked the steering wheel violently to his right. The little Yugo plunged into the hedge and grated to a stop, as the van blew past in the middle of the road.

Tweezer had his head down, studying the hand controls on his steering wheel, and by the time he looked up Finkter had already struggled out of the Yugo, and was jumping up and down in the middle of the road shaking his fist. He had never seen this vehicle before, and the driver was obviously an idiot. Finkter turned to look at his vehicle, the right wing of which was crushed into the hawthorn hedge.

"BOLLOCKS!" he shouted. He jumped back behind the wheel, and reached over his shoulder to shove the cardboard box back onto the backseat. He cranked the tiny engine back into life, found reverse, and floored the throttle. To his dismay, the front left wheel squirmed and spun on the asphalt while the right one whirled harmlessly in the ditch. Finkter pounded on the steering wheel, and screamed obscenities to himself, as the car vibrated on the spot.

By this time, Tweezer had reached the village, and was ready to try a few stops and starts to get used to the feel of the gearshift. He pulled over outside the Black Swan, performed a stilted three-point turn, and headed back toward the club. His first couple of efforts at pulling away from a standing start were less than successful, but gave him the opportunity to show off his vehicle and wave to some of the locals. After another jerky start, he pulled over outside St. Mungo's Parish Church, where the Reverend Merton Bulger was enjoying a Styrofoam cup of communion wine, and sunning himself on the bench outside. Tweezer rolled down the window and grinned at him.

"Hey, Rev," he yelled. "Look at me, I'm driving!"

The Reverend gave him the thumbs-up as he took off again.

Meanwhile, Finkter had managed to get the Yugo's four wheels back on the asphalt, by putting the car in reverse, wedging the throttle open with one of his shoes, and then sitting on the front of the car and bouncing up and down. Unfortunately, once the front wheels of the car had found purchase, it had rocketed backward, jettisoning Finkter, and burying its rear end in the opposite hedge. As Finkter gathered himself, he barely had time to dive out of the way of the same white van that had nearly killed him some moments before. He stumbled headfirst into the hedge as Tweezer blew by, and by the time he made it back behind the wheel of the Yugo, he was borderline rabid. The engine squealed into life once more, and he gunned the car forward, quickly catching up with the white van.

The van kept surging forward, braking and stopping, and then repeating the process. The road was much too narrow for Finkter to get in front, and the big policeman was now completely demented. He had extinct animals to plant, and photographic evidence to gather, and the last thing he needed was to be held up by some mentally retarded arsewipe like this. He hammered down on his horn, which gave a pitiful low raspberry sound, and then died altogether.

"BOLLOCKS!" he yelled. Then he leaned out of the window, shook his fist, and screamed, "Oi! You in front, pull over, you retard! I'm on urgent police business here!"

But there was no sign that the driver in front had heard him. "Bloody typical!" Finkter said to himself as the Yugo crawled along behind the van. He swerved from one side of the road to the other, craning his neck out of the side window to see if he could see a spot wide enough to pass. But there wasn't one.

"Isn't this bloody marvelous?" he muttered to himself. "Probably a Paki, or a woman. Or maybe a woman Paki.

"BOLLOCKS!" he yelled, pounding the steering wheel.

In front, Tweezer was getting better at his standing starts, and was far too excited to notice the car behind, with its occupant shaking his fist out the window. He was trying to balance the clutch and accelerator smoothly, so that he could make a stylish and triumphant return to the club, hopefully in front of Uncle Dickie. So far he hadn't got it quite right, but he was improving, he felt.

Behind, Finkter was going berserk, and was beside himself that he couldn't use his blue light and siren. Tweezer came to another halt in front of him, which was the final straw. Finkter got out of the car, slammed the door, and marched angrily toward the driver's side door. Just as he got within arm's length of the van, Tweezer pressed down on the accelerator again, and the van jumped off up the road. Finkter set off after it, yelling and shaking his fist, but gave up after about fifty yards, and sprinted back to his car. Every episode of *Starsky and Hutch* he had ever seen was spinning through his tiny mind as he jumped back behind the wheel.

"Obstruction of justice," he panted, as he gunned the Yugo off after the van. "And officer endangerment." He gripped the wheel feverishly, and caught up with Tweezer again, who was now slowing down for another try.

Tweezer heard a squeal of tires, as Finkter skidded to a halt a few feet behind him. He watched curiously in his wing mirror as the policeman jumped out of the car, pulled down his tunic, and straightened his helmet. Finkter angrily drew his nightstick, and he had every intention of using it, as he grasped the door

handle of the van and wrenched it open.

"What the hell do you think you're doing, you bastard!" he screamed at Tweezer, grabbing him by the collar with his left hand, and pulling him out so he could get a good swing at him with the nightstick. He didn't notice the wheelchair until it was too late, and the weight of it had toppled past the point of no return. Tweezer got his right hand on Finkter's throat as they all went down, and landed with a crash on the asphalt. Finkter hit the ground, as the right arm of the chair speared him in the crotch, tearing a large hole in his pants. He was in the process of doubling up in agony, with his face coming upward, when Tweezer landed flat on top of him, cannoning into his face, and driving his head back into the road once more. The chair bounced off into the road, leaving the two men in a heap.

Tweezer rolled off, and lay on his back in the road for a moment to catch his breath. Then slowly he pushed himself up into a sitting position, and dragged himself over to his chair, which was lying on its side, with one of its wheels turning slowly. He grabbed the wheel and pulled down, righting the chair, and then put the heels of his hands on the foot rest, reached one massive arm up and back to grasp a handlebar, and with a heave, hoisted himself back into a sitting position. Smiling to himself, he thought: Uncle Dickie was right. He picked up each of his legs, settled his feet onto the rest, and wheeled himself over to the prostrate figure of Finkter.

Now there's a man in bad shape, he thought. Finkter's jaw was obviously broken, he had a couple of teeth missing, and if the rip in his pants was anything to go by, when he woke up, he'd have to count his nuts before he rubbed them. Tweezer's only injury appeared to be a scrape on his left elbow, as he wheeled himself to the back of the van, opened the door, and hit the lift button. A few moments later, he pressed down on the accelerator one more time, engaged the clutch, and the van took off smoothly toward the club. "That's better," he said to himself, grinning, as he ran over Finkter's helmet.

A few moments later, Dwilby trotted by the scene with his nose in the air, testing the breeze. Whatever he was looking for was close. He gave Finkter a courtesy sniff, paying particular attention to his groin, and trotted on up the road. He stopped at the Yugo, and jumped up into the driver's seat. This was it. He could hear scratching in the back, coming from inside the box, which, after a couple of exploratory sniffs, he managed to nose open. He stared into the cage, with its one lifeless occupant, and a scurrying furry brown something. He sniffed around them both, and decided it was the dead one that had been in heat. He was a mongrel, but even he wouldn't go that low.

Dwilby hopped down from the car and trotted back toward the club, stopping only for another casual squirt, this time on Finkter's crotch. When he got back, Agnes was taking her nap and there was nobody around to mooch from. The only thing that interested him even slightly was the fact that the back door to the caddie wagon was open. He hopped up, and clambered over the golf bags and the piles of bedding and clothing, looking for something to eat. When he had satisfied himself that there was no food in the van, he settled on Flanagan's sleeping bag behind the driver's seat, rucked it up a little, and lay down for a nap.

CHAPTER TWELVE

Flanagan, Thirsty, Mills, and Boon were standing to attention behind Uncle Dickie's desk, paying close attention to the old man, as he used a pointer to describe the location of the Tay Club on a large map that he had pulled down on a roller from the wall behind him.

"The distilleries are here, here, and here," he said, turning to Thirsty and smiling. "Not today, Thirsty, if you could possibly manage it."

Thirsty grinned. "Absolutely no problem, sir."

"Thank you," said Uncle Dickie. "Now," as he returned to the map, "this golf course has only three holes, the first going out from the distillery at the McGregor compound, known as the 'Low House,' the second continuing in more or less the same direction, from the second distillery, the 'Light House,' and the third tee is on the point, right here." He pointed with a flourish. "The third distillery, the 'Last House,' is high on the bluff, over-looking the tee, and the hole goes back down the other side of the headland, finishing back at the McGregor compound."

"Excuse me, sir," said Ernie Mills, glancing out the window. "I think Tweezer's back."

Uncle Dickie walked over to the bay window, as Tweezer pulled up in the van. Tweezer grinned happily as Uncle Dickie beamed at him through the glass, and beckoned him to join them. "Isn't that a grand sight?" he said, as Tweezer let himself down on the lift, and pushed off toward the ramp to the veranda. Uncle Dickie sat down behind his desk, and a few moments later, there was a knock on the door, and Tweezer rolled in to join the line of men.

"How was it, son?" Uncle Dickie asked.

"As much fun as I've had for a long while, sir!"

"And the day's not done yet!" Uncle Dickie shot back, pointing a finger at him. "Here's what I need you to do. Go to Beamish's quarters, and look in his arms chest for me. There should be some black powder and blast caps in there. A half dozen caps, and a quarter ounce of powder should do us nicely."

Tweezer looked confused, but said, "Yes, sir," saluted, and wheeled around.

Uncle Dickie looked at the rest of his men. "All right, then, boys, is everyone clear on their roles here?"

"Yes, sir," said all four men. "Very well then," said Uncle Dickie. "Then let's boogie, as they say. I need everyone in their vehicles in five minutes. Flanagan, bring around the Bentley, if you please."

Hammy backed the horse trailer deftly into the narrow space between the farmhouse and the barn, and hopped nimbly out of the Land Rover.

"First things first," he said, as Stanley clambered out with his stuff. "Ah don't know about you, Stanley, but ah could eat the balls off a low-flyin' duck."

Stanley hadn't realized how hungry he was until Hammy shoved an enormous plate of sausages, eggs, and hot buttered toast in front of him and went upstairs. Stanley was shoveling the food down gratefully, when Hammy returned with a pile of clothing. He looked at Stanley, and tossed the clothes onto the chair behind him. "Ye should really change," he said. "And a wee bath wouldn't be a bad idea either, if ye don't mind me sayin' so."

Stanley looked embarrassed. "Sorry about that," he said.

"Och, don't worry," Hammy laughed, as he started to eat his own food. "Ah heard them celebratin' last night. An' then the next thing y'know, they're beatin' on ma door at three in the morning, all whiskeyed up, lookin' fer somebody."

"That was me," Stanley mumbled through a mouthful of toast and egg. "I escaped down the beach to Carnoustie."

"Aye," said Hammy. "Ah spotted ye escapin'. All the way back tae here."

"How come you're not with them?" said Stanley. "I mean, if you're related and everything."

"Well," Hammy sighed, "it's just that ah always had a hankerin' fer the finer things in life, ye know? Like hot water every now and then, and the occasional wumman?"

"Oh, yes," Stanley said, motioning out the window to the compound below, "I can see how that would be a problem down there." He took another mouthful of food. "Speaking of problems," he continued, "How am I going to put this thing back without them noticing me?"

"Ah was thinkin' about tha', Stanley," Hammy said, as he wiped the remainder of his egg off his plate with a piece of toast. "Ah've a load of firewood tae deliver to them, an' you can be sure they need it after tha' blaze last night. We'll take it

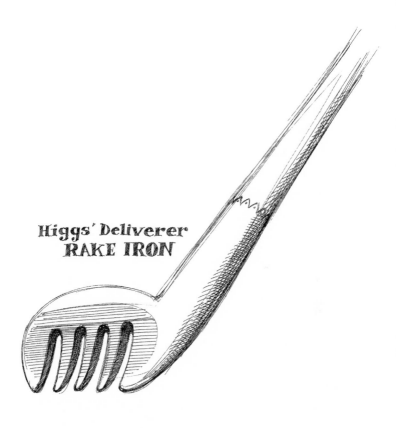

The Deliverer Rake Iron (Higgs, Robert P. *1905*).

Unlike the ordinary rake iron, the Deliverer, as shown, had its teeth facing downward, leaving gaps in the leading edge of the club. Despite a design concept that was tenuous at best, it received glowing recommendations from the likes of Harry Vardon and James Braid, both of whom used it "at least once" from sand and tall grass, but the colorful Viscount of Skegness once described it as being "about as much use as a trapdoor on a canoe."

In the early days of the last century, the average golfer was apparently less gullible than the infomercial-watching addict of today, and consequently these clubs are now highly collectible.

doon there in the horse box, an' maybe you can slip in there unnoticed tha' way."

"Yes," Stanley said, rubbing his chin. "But how do we get them to think it was never missing?"

"Okay, tha's a good pernt," Hammy said thoughtfully. "Y'll have tae take yer chances on it, but if y'can make sure whoever discovers it is the sort of dickhead who'd want to look clever, ye might have a chance."

The two men looked at each other across the table for a moment, and then simultaneously said, "Shuggie."

Finkter's eyelids flickered and then slowly opened. The sun was still low, but the sky was a piercing blue, and it was all he could see. He blinked, and slowly became aware of the pain, one area at a time. He reached up, gingerly touched his jaw, and flinched, which caused a stabbing pain in his groin. He rolled over onto one side, and drew up his knees. The back of his head was throbbing, and he felt as if a hedgehog might have taken up residence in his scrotum. Worse than that, he had obviously wet his pants. He groaned as he turned over and raised himself onto his hands and knees, a position from where, with great difficulty, he managed to stand up.

Finkter was too badly injured to be his usual angry self. He was sore all over and he was depressed. As he limped back to the Yugo, he tried to put together in his mind the events that had caused his current predicament and think of a course of action, but he couldn't. His mind simply wasn't big enough to deal with it. He reached the car, which was still running, and eased himself behind the wheel. In the back, the box was still there, and he could hear the scratching sounds of the surviving ferret.

Good, he thought. At least I still have that to look forward to. He leaned back as far in the seat as he could, and gently pushed his hand through the rip in his pants to hoist up his swollen genitals for the journey. One of his balls felt at least twice the size of the other, and for some reason, he could feel his heartbeat in it. "Ooh God," he squeaked. "That can't be good." He twisted the rearview mirror, and took a look at his face. Now he had a cut in his top lip too, and a couple of teeth, no, make that three teeth, missing. He returned the mirror to its position, reached over pain-fully to pull down his seat belt, and clicked it into the buckle. You can't be too careful, he thought to himself sarcastically. I mean, you wouldn't want to get into an accident, would you?

He put the little car into first gear, nosed it into the hedge, and then reversed, pausing to cough out a tooth that had lodged behind his swollen tongue. Then he carefully wiped his mouth on his sleeve and set off back through the village toward Nerdlington, and St. Egbert's Infirmary.

Uncle Dickie grasped the handle of the trapdoor under the Persian rug in his office, and heaved upward. The Maharajah looked on with interest as he leaned the door back on the wall, and started to descend into the secret basement.

"It's been a while since we were down here," he said, following Uncle Dickie down into the darkness.

"Yes, indeed," said Uncle Dickie, as he fumbled with the

light switch. The room fluttered into fluorescent light, and Uncle Dickie's treasures were revealed. One side of the room was a wall of wine, filled with rare Château Yquem and ancient Margaux, bottles of Louis XIII Cognac, and prehistoric Ports. Two Renoirs, a Chagall, and several Magrittes adorned the back wall, and on the left, the wall was a series of bank vault doors.

Uncle Dickie polished his reading glasses with his handkerchief, put them on, and began to turn the knobs on the first safe. After a few moments, he pulled the great handle down with a clang, and swung the heavy door open.

It was considerably cooler in the vault, and Uncle Dickie shivered as he started pulling out metal drawers.

"It's rather like a small morgue, Dickie," the Maharajah said from the portal. "You know, you're exhuming your little mummies down here."

"Except, of course," said Uncle Dickie, as he removed a long, slim leather sleeve from one of the drawers, "these are not mummified." He unsheathed an elegant-looking hickory-shafted golf club, and handed it to Poony. "They are, as you can see, perfectly preserved."

The Maharajah waggled the club, which was a strange looking iron, with downward facing teeth. "It's in wonderful condition, Dickie," he said, "but what the hell is it for?"

Uncle Dickie took the club, and began putting it back into its sleeve. "Actually," he said, "this one never really caught on, although it did serve a worthwhile purpose. It's a Deliverer Rake Iron, made by Robert P. Higgs, around the turn of the century. The teeth would just stick in the ground, and twist the head offline, often breaking the shaft, but there are some situations in which it may prove useful."

He looked at the Maharajah with a wink. "An example that has never been hit, like this one, is incredibly valuable. "However," he continued, "there are a number of other clubs down here, in equally good condition, that could prove invaluable over the next couple of days, and I am going to take them with me." He began pulling out drawers, and removing the leather sleeves, which he tucked under his arm.

"But Dickie," the Maharajah said, with a look of consternation on his face. "These clubs are worth a fortune, surely you are not going to risk causing damage to them?"

"Oh, yes, I am," said Uncle Dickie, as he clambered over the portal with an armful of clubs. "Because they deserve to see the heat of battle at least once. They were meant to be used, and I have waited a long time for the right occasion upon which to use them!" He slammed the door and spun the dials.

"Speaking of things that were meant to be used," he said, as he made his way over to the wine wall. "Hmm, let me see." He reached up and pulled out a bottle. "Yquem 'Twenty-one," he mumbled to himself. "That ought to be about ready, what do you think, Poony? Perhaps we'd better take a half case."

"It's more than seventy years old," replied the Maharajah, "It should be good."

"No, I meant 1821, Poony. Botrytis, and the old noble rot! It should be either great or completely undrinkable. Grab another five bottles, old boy, and follow me. Let's get this show on the road."

Flanagan had the motor of the caddie wagon running, and he was drumming his fingers on the steering wheel. He looked at his wristwatch. "What the hell are they doing, Thirsty?" he asked.

Thirsty sat in the passenger seat, cracking his knuckles. "I dunno, but I need to get up there, Seamus," he said. "It's been an hour now and I'm beginning to get antsy."

Flanagan looked at him seriously. "Aye," he said. "Ah can see the fog liftin' from ye, all right. Yer eyes are startin' to look a wee bit evil."

"No kidding, pal, wait a minute, here they come!"

Uncle Dickie was carrying what looked like a trombone case and was walking purposefully with the Maharajah, across the gravel toward his shining black Bentley Turbo 8, which Flanagan had parked outside his office. He opened the back door, slid the case in, and walked over to the passenger's side of the caddie wagon to speak to Flanagan and Thirsty.

Thirsty stiffened as he poked his head through the window.

"Follow me, Flanagan," he said, "until we hit the main road to Newcastle. Then I'm going to floor it. We will rendezvous at the Aberfeldy Palace Hotel at fourteen hundred hours. Got it?"

"Yes, sir," said Flanagan.

Uncle Dickie walked back to the Bedford van, where Mills and Boon were sitting alongside Tweezer, who was excitedly explaining the controls to the vehicle. They all sat up a little straighter as he approached.

"Follow Flanagan, men," he said, and looking at Tweezer with a wink, "And don't spare the horses!"

Uncle Dickie settled himself behind the wheel of the Bentley, and took a deep breath. "Well, Poony, here we go!" he said, as the tires chewed a little gravel, then bit hard, and the big car surged out of the courtyard and onto Hadrian's Lane. The yellow Volkswagen and the Bedford followed, and some minutes later, the convoy was cruising through the village, where most of the local population had turned out to wave and cheer as they went by. Uncle Dickie beamed as he waved back. "No secrets in this town," he laughed.

Once they had gone through the village, the road once again turned narrow for a while, until it T-junctioned into the main road, which passed through the town of Nerdlington and snaked on through the moors, to Newcastle-upon-Tyne.

Uncle Dickie stopped at the T-junction, and looked left and right, as the Maharajah tightened his seat belt and lit up a Turkish cigarette. "Allah be praised," he said and then crossed himself for good measure. Uncle Dickie turned right slowly, and then, once the car was in line, he stamped brutally on the throttle.

"Oooh, my living jungle hat!" the Maharajah yelled, as the Bentley fishtailed wildly, before its massive soft-compound Bridgestones found purchase, and catapulted the car forward like a jet fighter. "Curry my dog, Dickie, what the hell have you done to this thing?" the Maharajah howled, as his turban fell of the back of his head.

Uncle Dickie was in his element. "I had Mills tweak her a little," he yelled, over the roar of the turbo-charged V-8, as the speedometer hit third gear at eighty-five, and the car gave another frightening rush forward. "Almost eight hundred horsepower now!"

The Bentley was doing a hundred and thirty miles per hour, and had just dropped into fourth gear, when they blew past a little Yugo that had maxed out at forty, on the long straightaway into Nerdlington. Finkter, who had been lost in his own painful little daydream, did not notice the Bentley coming, and the turbulence that it created on its way past almost blew him off the road and into the ditch. He had just pulled himself together again, when he was passed by a beaten-up yellow Volkswagen, followed by a white Bedford panel van, both of which were also speeding.

CHAPTER THIRTEEN

From the kitchen window, Stanley trained a pair of field glasses across the little inlet onto the McGregor compound, a couple of hundred feet below. Hamish had the clan lined up beside the smoking remains of the bonfire, and was walking up and down the line, gesticulating wildly, and obviously pitching a fit. Hammy stood beside Stanley with his hands in his pockets.

"Ah remember Hamish when he was relatively normal," he said.

"Oh yes?" said Stanley. "What changed that?"

"Not what," said Hammy. "Who... I mean it wuz a wumman, ye know? Ah'm Hamish's brother," he said, as he pulled a chair from the kitchen table over to the window and sat down. His eyes glazed over. "Her name wuz Bridget, an' she had to choose between the two of us, nearly forty years ago this December."

Stanley put the field glasses on the windowsill and turned to face Hammy. "I don't see her with Hamish," he smiled.

"Aye, an' ye don't see her wi' me either, do ye?" said Hammy, his breath steaming up the window.

Stanley looked remorseful. "I'm sorry," he said. "What happened?"

Hammy got up and walked over to the mantelpiece, and took a photograph down. He handed it to Stanley. It was in color, but badly faded, and Stanley could just make out the face of a woman with her arm around Hammy. She was smiling, and Hammy looked embarrassed.

"She died," Hammy said.

"Oh, God, Hammy," said Stanley. "I'm so sorry. How long ago?"

"Nineteen years, four months, and eleven days. She was on the Pier in Arbroath with tha' bastard down there," Hammy spat. "An' she fell in, or so the story goes. Wasn't a swimmer. Funny thing wuz, though, she'd left me a few hours earlier t'tell Hamish tha' she wuz gonna marry me."

Stanley didn't know what to say, so he just looked at the floor. Hammy got up, and started to pull on his coat. "Ah'll tell ye what, Stanley," he said. "Ah see no reason why ye should go down there at all. There's no way they'll suspect anything from me. Givvus yer wee box, an' ah'll be back here in no time."

It was a busy day in the emergency room at St. Egbert's Infirmary. Finkter sat in the waiting room with a cross section of the local society he hated so vehemently. He had been there for almost an hour now, and there were still three people ahead of him in line, an old man with a gigantic eye patch, a screaming toddler with a self-tapping screw stuck up his nose, and a Nigerian woman who had apparently cut herself shaving. He had lied about his injuries to the admissions clerk, and he was praying that he would get a white, male doctor. At this stage, he didn't even care if the guy was Jewish.

Finally, his name was called; but, to his dismay, he was summoned by the pretty young blonde doctor he had been watching all morning as she did her rounds in her fishnet stockings and high heels, with her clipboard and silver pen.

"James Finkter? Mr. James Finkter, with a sprained ankle?"

Finkter heard a couple of sniggers, as he got up and limped after her, as she walked past reception, and into the treatment area. She flung back a flimsy curtain and motioned for Finkter to sit on the bed. "Which ankle was it, sir, she said, smiling, until she noticed his face. Finkter did his best impression of a smile, which made him look like he was trying not to fart. "Well, doctor," he said, "Ah, this is a little embarrassing. You see, it's not so much my ankle, but, well, er, it's the old wedding tackle, so to speak." He giggled nervously.

She cut in, "Well, I see, but..."

"No," Finkter said. "You really have to see it. One of my testicles is huge, and my whole sack is filled with fluid. Look." He reached in through the tear in his trousers, and gingerly produced his scrotum, which had now swollen to about half the size of a grapefruit. "You see?"

The doctor seemed transfixed at the sight, and for a moment, Finkter thought she was going to scream. "What's wrong?" he asked. "Surely you must see this sort of thing all the time?"

"No, I don't," she said, taking a step backward out of the cubicle. "I'm just an admissions clerk. The doctor will be with you in a moment." She pulled the curtain across, and made a hasty retreat.

Finkter sat down on the edge of the bed again, and stared blankly ahead. A few moments later the curtains were drawn once more, and an enormous West Indian woman appeared. "Mr. Finkter!" she said cheerfully, extending her hand. "I'm Doctor La' Trina N'Dildwe, and I believe you have something to show me!"

Tweezer, Mills, and Boon were cruising along nicely behind the caddie wagon in the new Bedford, listening to U2 on the radio. Like Tweezer, neither Carson Mills, nor Charlie Boon had served Uncle Dickie, but both were men whom the old man felt had been treated unfairly by the armed forces. The subject of gays in the military made Uncle Dickie feel uncomfortable, and he didn't like to talk about it much. He felt it enough to say that he had seen enough hatred in the world and couldn't think of a reason to persecute two people who loved one another, provided they left everyone else alone.

Both Mills and Boon had been dishonorably discharged from the British armies, despite exemplary records, and Uncle Dickie had been quick to jump to their defense. In the process, he had made himself extremely unpopular at the Ministry of Defense, which had been hoping the problem would just go away. During the Falklands campaign, Mills, who was a world-class shot, had been among the first paratroopers to be dropped in. From three-quarter mile range, and under heavy fire, he had pinned down an entire company of Argentinean troops for long enough to allow several British families to be evacuated.

His partner Boon was a brilliant engineer, who had served in the engine room of a destroyer, which had been hit below the waterline in the same theater. Boon had spent twenty minutes in the icy south Atlantic, bringing three other sailors out through the hole, two of them mortally wounded. Uncle Dickie didn't care that they were gay. To him they were soldiers, and two of the best he had ever seen. "They are the type of men," Uncle Dickie said in a rare, and somewhat unfortunate choice of words, "that a Queen and her country should be proud of."

"In the name of love," Tweezer wailed tunelessly, grinning at the two men to his left. Boon laughed. "Bloody hell, Tweeze," he said, covering his ears. "Yeah," Mills chipped in, "Leave it to Bono, fer gawd's sake."

But Tweezer was too happy to be insulted. "I wonder what the boys in front are up to," he said, pointing at the caddie wagon. He peered over the steering wheel, looking a little closer. "Oh crikey," he said, squinting even harder. "Do you see what I see?"

Mills and boon sat forward a little, and looked at the back window of the yellow Volkswagen. Dwilby was perched on a suitcase, and had steamed up a corner of the back window with his breath.

In the caddie wagon ahead, Flanagan turned to Thirsty. "That *is* you," he said. "It's the third time ah've smelt it now, so it can't be comin' from outside."

"And for the third time, Seamus," said Thirsty, "I'm telling you it wasn't me. My system doesn't have enough nourishment in it to create a fart like that. It must be you. Maybe you've lost control, you know? They're slippin' out unnoticed."

Flanagan's cell phone rang.

"Hello?"

"It's Tweezer," Flanagan said to Thirsty. "What was that, Tweeze?"

Flanagan turned around and shoved the duffel bag behind his

head sideways. "Oh, ma God, Thirsty… Agnes is going to kill me." he said.

Thirsty looked back, and then at Flanagan, with a hurt expression. "Go on then, apologize."

Hammy bounced in the seat of the Land Rover as he drove down the rough track toward the compound. In the horse trailer behind, the digit was bundled up in a stack of kindling beside the rest of the firewood, and, as luck would have it, Hamish was still roasting the boys over by the remains of the bonfire, when he parked in front of Shuggie's hut. Quickly he jumped out, and ran around the back to let the door down. He pulled on the string that bound the kindling together, grabbed the box, and keeping the horse box between himself and the clan, he nipped inside the hut, and hid it beside the stove, where Shuggie would see it the first time he stoked the fire. Then he jumped back into the Land Rover, and with the door to the trailer still down, stamped on the accelerator. With a crash like thunder, the pile of wood inside came tumbling out, and spread out across the mud. Hammy got out slowly, and waved across to Hamish, who was now staring at him.

"Here's yer wood, Hamish!" he yelled, as he closed the door to the trailer. And under his breath as he climbed back behind the wheel, "An' ah hope ye burn with it, ye black-hearted bastard."

Up on the side of the hill, Stanley was watching from the window. Hammy bounced down the track and back onto the asphalt, and a few moments later, he almost ran over Stanley, who was waiting for him in the driveway. He clambered out of the cab.

"Part One of Plan A is complete, Stanley!" he announced.

"Yess!" Stanley shouted, with both fists in the air. "How can I ever repay you, Hammy?"

"Let's just go an' watch," said Hammy. "Tha' might be enough."

Shuggie was exhausted, monumentally hung over, and freezing his tits off. He was trudging back to his hut, with every intention of collapsing into bed, when he heard Hamish scream from behind, "Hey, fat boy! You can pick up tha' wood, and bring me a stack of it as quick as ye like!"

Perfect, Shuggie thought. Up all night drinking lighter fluid and then forced to climb up and down hills in the freezing darkness, looking for some dickhead with one nut. Followed by a little aerobic exercise and splinters. Perfect. He gathered up an armful of wood, and blundered into his hut, colliding with the door, and dropping the wood all over the place. He picked up a couple of stray logs, opened the door to his stove, and froze.

"Where the bollocks did tha' come from?" he said to himself, out loud.

Over the next few seconds, Shuggie's mind performed a complicated series of computations, resulting in the belief that somehow *he* must have been responsible for the location of the box. It was the only logical explanation. He had been drinking last night, but not as much as Hamish, who had just torn him about seven new arseholes, in front of the rest of the men, and had been unkind enough to suggest that they would come in useful, given the amount of shite that he produced. Shuggie must have taken the box from his Chieftain last night, and placed it here for safekeeping.

Shuggie was hurt. Shuggie was more sensitive than people thought. Shuggie was a *genius*!

He grabbed the box, barged out the door and barreled over to Hamish's hut with it. He knocked politely on the door.

"Oh, Hamish," he sang. "It's me, Shuggie!"

Hamish, who was not feeling exactly wonderful either this morning, got up off his bed and stumbled to the door. "What?" he snapped, opening it and glaring at Shuggie, who stood there, smirking like a kilted Oliver Hardy, drumming his fat fingers on the box. Hamish stared at it, for a moment speechless.

"A wee prezzie," said Shuggie smarmily. "From the big fat, *stupid* clansman, okay?"

Hamish was looking at the box as if it were filled with dynamite.

"Honestly," said Shuggie. "It's fer you. Ah had a wee bit too much tae drink last night, Hamish, unlike yerself, of course, an' ah fergot that ah put it away fer safekeeping when you fell over backward an' pished yerself on ma floor, ye know?"

Hamish took the box, opened it a little, peered inside, and looked back at Shuggie, who was obviously waiting for something. "Aye, well," he started. "Ah suppose ah owe ye an apology, Shug," he mumbled, reddening under his beard, and staring at Shuggie suspiciously.

Shuggie feigned deafness and cupped his ear.

"Sorry, Hamish, wha' wis tha'?"

Hamish glared at him. "Don't push it, Shuggie," he said. "Well done. Now go an' get some sleep."

Shuggie saluted and said, "Okay, then. See ye later!" and skipped off back toward his hut. Back up the hill, Stanley let out a whoop, put down the field glasses, and tried to give Hammy a high five, missing his hand altogether. Seconds later, he was on the telephone.

"Well done, Beamish!" said Uncle Dickie. He and the Maharajah were driving through Dundee and Stanley was on speakerphone.

"Sir," Stanley said excitedly. "If you make a left at the train station in Carnoustie and follow the road on around, you'll come to Hammy's house without the McGregors' seeing you. We have a perfect view of the compound from up here, and there's a barn if you want to stash the Bentley."

"Splendid work, my boy," Uncle Dickie laughed. "That's exactly the kind of stuff I need from you. The Maharajah and I are going to stop at the hotel in just a moment, and we will probably stay here, considering the weather, but I expect Flanagan and the boys will see you around sixteen hundred hours."

"Very good, sir," said Stanley. "Hammy and I will be here."

Uncle Dickie hit the end button, and turned to the Maharajah, who was shaking his head and smiling.

"What?"

Poonsavvy stared at him, incredulous.

"You, my old friend, are unbelievable."

"Maybe," said Uncle Dickie. "But did you hear his voice?

He's grown a foot today, I guarantee it."

Finkter had spent four hours at the hospital, and was now taped, drained, and wired, in more ways than one. Dr. N'Dildwe had given him a prescription for Percodan, which Finkter thought was an antibiotic. His jaw was wired shut, and he had been told that he was probably not going to be able to eat anything solid for about ten days, so what the hell, he thought, I might as well drink lunch. He needed a couple of stiff snorts anyway; I mean what kind of a friggin' morning was that?

He sat behind his desk and looked at the yellow pills. The doctor had given him one at the hospital, and it didn't seem that it had done him much good. He thought they were probably a little small, so he forced two more of them behind his molars, and onto his tongue, and washed them down with a couple of large swigs from the bottle of brandy in his drawer.

Twenty minutes later, he felt no pain. In fact, he felt like Captain Fantastic. It was all he could do to restrain himself from pulling on a pair of Y-fronts over his trousers, sticking out his arm, shouting, "God save the Queen!" at the top of his voice, and flying down the main street.

Now, he thought, where did I put those gerbils?

CHAPTER FOURTEEN

The manager of the Aberfeldy Palace Hotel opened the door to the Trossachs Suite and stood back to allow the Maharajah and Uncle Dickie to enter.

A bellman struggled after them with two large Louis Vuitton trunks, which he set down heavily. "A bedroom and bathroom ensuite on this side, sirs," said the manager, "And the same over here, with this being the lounge."

Uncle Dickie took a look around. "Thank you, my good man," he said. "This will do splendidly." He slipped the bellman a five-pound note on his way out.

"Well, Poony old boy," Uncle Dickie said, as he walked over to the window, and pulled back the sheers. Rain smacked hard against the panes, and a hundred feet below, the firth was boiling against the rocks, while the sky had turned an angry blue-black. "Tough day to be a seagull!"

"Yes," said the Maharajah, rummaging in his trunk, and pulling out a lilac silk robe. "I can't believe these people wear kilts up here!"

Uncle Dickie picked up his trunk, heaved it through into the bedroom, and opened it on the bed. Auntie Myrtle had packed for him, and the first thing he noticed was a little heart-shaped bar of chocolate on top of his neatly folded tweed trousers. He smiled and began to unpack.

At two o'clock, they made their way down to the drawing room, and ordered tea and sandwiches. They sat by the window to eat and watched as the weather grew more violent. Flanagan and the boys were a little late when they pulled into the parking lot. The Maharajah watched from inside, as Uncle Dickie struggled down the granite steps with a golf umbrella, and issued his latest orders to the men. They drove off, as he scampered back up the steps and reappeared in the drawing room, looking a little flustered. He sat down heavily, smoothed his silver hair back, and wiped the moisture off his face with a handkerchief.

"Where are the men staying tonight?" asked the Maharajah.

Uncle Dickie winced a little as he said, "Well, I hate to do it to them, but I really need them in position tonight, to keep an eye on the McGregors. Hamish will be expecting me, I'm sure, and God knows what trickery he has planned."

"You're not saying they have to camp out on a night like this?"

"It's not going to be like this tonight, Poony," Uncle Dickie said as he walked across the room and sat down by the window that faced the firth. "It's forecast to blow through. What worries me is the Haar."

"The what?"

"The Haar. It's a layer of marine air, a blanket of mist that rolls in off the North Sea every now and then up here. If the wind dies tonight, conditions are perfect for it."

He stroked his chin and twisted the ends of his mustache as he walked back over to sit down beside the Maharajah. "I've been waiting for this match for half a century, Poony, and it would be a cruel twist of fate if the weather were to rob me of a fair chance of winning it. All I want is a level battlefield upon which to fight. We have the McGregors thinking that the match is their idea and we come reluctantly, which is perfect." He stood up and put his hands in his pockets. "I'm not worried about us," he said, looking a little vexed. "But I would like to be able to see what *they* are up to."

The windshield wipers on the Volkswagen were pitifully inadequate to deal with the vicious squalls that were sweeping in from the North Sea. Flanagan could barely see the road in front of him at times, and was crawling at a snail's pace. Behind, the high sides of the Bedford were a problem for Tweezer too, The van was being buffeted and rocked offline by the breeze, and Mills and Boon were secretly glad to be going so slowly behind Flanagan. Given his recent lack of experience behind the wheel, Tweezer was doing a pretty good job, and they told him so. It was close to four o'clock, and unnaturally dark, as the two vehicles pulled into Hammy's lane and bounced down toward the farmhouse.

Stanley stood under the porch and waved energetically, as they pulled up outside. He opened a small black umbrella and ran out to meet Flanagan. Almost instantly, it was blown inside out, and he retreated under the porch again. Flanagan and Thirsty tumbled into the house, wiping their faces, and were followed by Mills and by Boon, pushing Tweezer. Stanley set about introducing everyone to Hammy, who was pouring boiling water into the teapot.

"Make yerselves at home, lads," he said, as the men sat at the kitchen table, blowing into their hands and rubbing them together. Thirsty was on his hands and knees, and had opened every drawer in Hammy's sideboard.

"Ahem," Hammy coughed, as he watched him tearing out napkins, books, and a box of cutlery. Thirsty ignored him, and carried on rummaging.

"Oh aye," Flanagan said. "Sorry about Thirsty, Hammy, but if he doesn't get a drink in the next few minutes, he's probably goin' to have to kill somethin'."

Hammy looked at the tiny man on the floor. "Ooh, ah see,' he said. "Well, tha's a wee bit of a problem. You see, ah nivver touch the stuff."

Thirsty stood up and appeared to be thinking. The rest of the men looked alarmed.

"Steady, wee man," Flanagan said. "We'll get it dealt with."

Thirsty said nothing, but marched to the door, flung it open with a clatter, and headed out into the storm. Everyone gathered on the porch to watch, including Hammy, who was still holding the kettle.

"Oh shite," said Flanagan, as Thirsty wrenched open the back door of the caddie wagon, and pulled out a yellow plastic poncho. Flanagan watched in horror, as Dwilby shot out, shook himself violently, and took off like a bullet through a five-bar gate into a herd of sheep that had huddled against the stone wall. "Oh, double shite," Flanagan said, as the animals scattered.

Thirsty pulled on the poncho, hopped over the wall, and marched off into the teeth of the wind. Stanley looked at Flanagan, who had turned a deathly shade of white. "Does he know where the distilleries are?" he asked.

"Aye," said Flanagan, who was watching Dwilby tearing

around the field, nipping at the sheep and barking. "He does."

Hammy ushered the men back inside and closed the door. "Well, Stanley," he said with a look of amusement. "Things have livened up a wee bit roon' here since you showed up!"

Stanley put his hand over his mouth and shook his head. "Sorry about your sheep, Hammy."

Hammy looked surprised. "Och, nivver wurry yerself, son. Those're Hamish's! It's the wee man ah'd be concerned fer. The boys have a guard on all of those stills."

Flanagan held his head in his hands.

"Oooh, triple shite!"

Thirsty tramped down the hill, toward the sea. When he had heard that his services would not be required until the morning, his natural instincts had kicked in. He needed a drink in the worst possible way. He had seen *The Perfect Storm*, and it didn't frighten him nearly as much as the thought of being sober for a minute longer than he had to. Lights glimmered in the windows, but the compound was deserted, as he marched past Hamish's hut and on toward the first tee and the long, low, thatched building behind it.

On this particular evening, it was the great misfortune of Stuart McGregor to be on duty, as the door to the distillery burst open, and Thirsty barged in. Stuart had his feet up on the table and was leaning back in his chair, as Thirsty, without breaking stride, kicked the back legs out from under him. Stuart barely had time to register surprise, before the back of his head hit the floor, and his lights went out. Thirsty continued on into the building until he reached the first vat, whereupon he immediately lay down on his back and positioned his mouth under the outlet valve. He reached up, eased it open, and, without swallowing, allowed about a pint of the fiery liquid to flow down his throat. Then he got up, steadied himself, and went to find something more portable.

Stuart had staggered to his feet, and was shaking his head, just as Thirsty walked back into the office with a case of malt on his right shoulder. The last thing Stuart remembered about that evening was a case of malt, rushing toward his nose at the speed of light. Twenty minutes later, Thirsty was panting as he slammed the case down on Hammy's kitchen table. He grinned.

"Sorry about that, boys," he said, taking a knife from the table and jimmying off the wooden lid. He looked at Flanagan. "Seamus, why the long face?"

"Dwilby's gone."

Flanagan knew that Agnes would go berserk when she found out that Dwilby was missing, and God only knew what the consequences might be, if anything happened to the dog. But there were even more pressing matters to attend to, so the caddies met around the kitchen table and discussed Uncle Dickie's orders.

"The old man wants us in position before daybreak so that we can monitor the McGregors' movements early," Flanagan said. "Tweeze, you'll be on the auxiliary bag, an' I'll take the Hogans as usual. Thirsty, he wants you an' Mills workin' forward, with you lookin out fer his ball, an' Mills keepin' an eye on McGregor's. The Maharajah will be an observer only, an' has expressed his desire to be left out of any altercation, but ye know what'll happen if push comes to shove. Boon, you will run interference, and take up early positions at each of the distilleries." He turned to look at Thirsty. "Tha' is, if there's anything left in the first one. Wee man, ye have t'be straightened up by the mornin', okay?"

Thirsty took a swig from his bottle, and burped loudly. "No problem, Seamus. I'm yer man."

"Okay then," Flanagan said, looking out the window at the dim lights of the compound below. The wind was dying, and the rain had subsided considerably. Hammy joined Flanagan at the window, and said, "Ye know there'll be a Haar the morrow, don't ye?"

Flanagan looked puzzled. "What's a Haar?" he asked.

"Oh, you'll see," said Hammy. "Or rather, ye won't."

Flanagan's phone rang in his pocket, and he fished it out. "Ooh, hullo, wee pet," he said, his eyes growing wider.

Thirsty turned to Stanley, grimaced, and said, "Ooh dearie me."

The men listened to one side of the conversation, and watched Flanagan squirm.

"Yes, petal," he cooed. "Ah was just about to call ye, because we discovered the wee fella in the back of the caddie wagon when we got here." He held the phone at arm's length for a few seconds and winced. "Ooh, he's doin' fine, an enjoyin' a wee bit of a change in the scenery, if his antics are anythin' to go by.

Yes, dear. Hold on a sec, ah'll get him."

Flanagan covered the mouthpiece and hissed at Boon, "Charlie, bark like a dog fer me!"

Boon almost choked on a sip of tea, and ran his fingers through his tousled mop of hair.

"Seamus!" he said coyly, "I had no idea you felt that way about me!"

Flanagan looked like he was about to burst into flames as he covered the mouthpiece again and begged for anyone in the room to help. Thirsty almost peed in his pants, as Boon got down on the floor, and started to woof energetically.

"There ye go, sweet pea," Flanagan said with relief, "Just listen to the wee man, he's havin' a great time!" Boon put his arm around Flanagan and started to snuffle and growl around the mouthpiece, as Flanagan tried in vain to struggle free.

"Aye, he certainly is a wee monkey, yes, yes, aye, ah'll give him a goodnight kiss from his mammy, yes, dear, now you have a good night now an' don't worry about a thing."

Flanagan put the phone in his pocket as Boon let him go, and pursed his lips, as if to kiss him.

"Ooh, very funny," said Flanagan, snatching the bottle from Thirsty, and taking a huge swig.

Flanagan was thinking that Thirsty's foray to the distillery might have alerted the McGregors to the imminent arrival of Uncle Dickie, but, as it happened, he needn't have worried.

The rain was falling softly, and the wind had all

but disappeared, when Hamish heard the soft knocking on his door. Uncle Dickie stood in the drizzle, wearing a Burberry raincoat and a deerstalker hat. Without a word, Hamish beckoned him inside. Uncle Dickie took off his hat, and shook it. He peered around the dimly lit interior.

"Love what you've done with the place, Hamish," he said.

Hamish sat down in an old wooden rocking chair, stroked Brenna, and began to fill his pipe. "Cut the crap, Gussett," he said. "We both know what's goin' on here. You an' me tomorrow at dawn, hand to hand, and this time it's on mah turf. If ye win, ye can take the Digit back, an' there'll be no more said."

"Yes," said Uncle Dickie. "Original rules, play the ball as it lies, and the course as you find it?"

Hamish pulled on his pipe several times and blew a large smoke ring at Uncle Dickie.

"Is there any other way?"

"No," said Uncle Dickie. "I don't believe there is." He pulled on his hat, bade Hamish good evening, and tramped across the mud and onto the beach. He picked his way between huge pieces of seaweed-festooned driftwood that had been tossed up by the storm, down to the water's edge, and gazed out across the firth, to the twinkling lights of St. Andrews. The sky was clearing, and the moon spilled a shaft of silver light onto the water, as he raised his arms, closed his eyes, and whispered, "Yesss."

Inside the hut, Hamish was lying on his bed, with a cell phone to his ear. "Stanford," he said. "We're on fer the morrow." He listened for a few seconds, hit End, and slid the phone back under his pillow.

Finkter had managed to control himself until darkness had fallen, by drinking heavily and building a scale model of the clubhouse out of Legos? There was even a small tan and white dog. Dr. N'Dildwe had wired his jaw with a mesh across his teeth, forcing his mouth into a position that had left him with a permanent robotic grin. He still had eight of the little yellow pills left, a couple of which he had popped just a few minutes earlier, and now he was feeling positively invincible. Sir Stanford had called earlier that afternoon to see how things were going, and Finkter thought that their conversation had gone swimmingly. He had told him that the powers at large in the golf club were considerably more organized than he had first suspected, and planting the animals was going to take just a little more time. Sir Stanford had suggested that they meet again that evening, shortly after sundown, at the Black Swan.

Finkter pulled on a black ski mask, slipped a hip flask of brandy into his back pocket, and carried the model of the clubhouse over to the back door of the Police Station, where he carefully placed it on the floor. Then he opened the door and peeked out left and right. The coast was clear, so he jumped out dramatically, with both his hands raised in an exaggerated karate chop position. He was in plainclothes this time, dressed in black from head to foot, as both of his uniforms had been destroyed, the first by a man with one leg and the second by a man in a wheelchair. None of this even occurred to him as he reached in, picked up the model, closed the door with his heel, and crept sideways, ninja-style, up the alley. The narcotic painkillers and the shots of brandy had elevated his senses to an almost mystic level of consciousness, where he felt like he was having one of those out-of-body experiences he had read about in the *National Enquirer*. Not even the drain the doctor had taped into his scrotum was giving him any cause for concern, as he hugged the back wall of the Black Swan and slipped into the kitchen. No knocking on doors. This time he would just materialize in front of Sir Stanford, like in *Star Trek*.

Sir Stanford was deep in conversation with Nigel Oglesby, and Sammy Mellon was behind the bar as usual, standing with his back toward Finkter, as the policeman crept into the bar.

"McGregor and his men will look after the procurement of the 'merchandise' he has with him up there," Sir Stanford was whispering to Oglesby.

Finkter stood with his feet apart, holding the Lego model, and boomed, "GREETINGSH, MEN!" at the top of his voice.

Sammy Mellon almost jumped out of his skin, and dropped a pint glass with a smash into the sink in front of him. He patted his heart, and turned to face Finkter, who was doing a splendid impersonation of a spaced-out, masked Legomaniac with metal teeth.

Finkter pulled off the mask, and swaggered over to the bar, where he slapped the speechless Mellon on the back. "Shorry about the appearansh, Mellon, but thingsh have got a little more sherioush around here." He put the model down on the table, and turned to Oglesby and Sir Stanford, thrusting out his hand. "Shtan, Nige, good to shee you men here. Letsh talk."

Sir Stanford looked incredulously at Oglesby and then back at Finkter, who folded his arms on the table and put his chin on his hands. Then Finkter looked in through the front door of the clubhouse, and started to hum the theme from *Mission Impossible*.

"Oh dear," said Oglesby.

Sir Stanford stood up, and put his arm around Oglesby's shoulder. "Finkter old boy, will you excuse Oglesby and me for just one moment?"

Finkter looked up. "Oh shertainly, Shtan," he said, and went back to playing with the model.

Sir Stanford ushered Oglesby back into the kitchen, and whispered at him, "What the hell is up with him?"

Oglesby looked over Sir Stanford's shoulder, back out to the bar, where Mellon was watching, as Finkter flew the Lego Dwilby over the roof of the clubhouse and made machine-gun sounds. "I'm buggered if I know," he said. "Perhaps he's flipped."

"Oh no," Sir Stanford hissed sarcastically, looking behind him. "Do you really think so? I mean he's out there playing with Lego, and pretending a plastic dog is an F-Sixteen. Seems perfectly normal to me."

Oglesby leaned on the edge of the stove, and pursed his lips. "Hmm," he said. "You know, there's probably still a way to make this work. I mean, with Gussett and the curry-muncher gone, the only people we have to worry about are a bunch of cripples and drunks. We could use Finkter as a diversion, and you and I could drop the ferrets and take the pictures."

Sir Stanford drew a deep breath, and shook his head. "I don't know," he said anxiously. "I really can't be seen here. The scandal would be horrific if I were to be placed at the scene, never

mind implicated."

"Yes," said Oglesby, with a smarmy grin, as he sauntered over to the doorway, and stood with his hands in his pockets. He put his pudgy face in front of Sir Stanford's. "But just how badly do you want those clubs?"

"Oh, I want them badly, Oglesby," he growled. "I want them sooo badly. The greatest antique golf club collection in the world must be put back into the possession of those people who understand its potential to destroy the sanctity of the rules of golf. We need to destroy them shaft by shaft, hosel by hosel, and face by face before the evil manufacturers begin replicating them by the truckful and placing these Godless tools into the bags of every duffer, skuller, and hacker in the world!" Sir Stanford quivered violently, in sudden realization that he'd grabbed hold of Oglesby's throat and was seconds away from snuffing the life out of his only reasonable co-conspirator.

Nigel gasped as Sir Stanford led him back to the table and had Mellon bring him a pint of beer.

"So, Sergeant Finkter," Sir Stanford said. "Tell us what you have planned for this evening." Then he threw his arms in the air, and walked to the other side of the bar, where he leaned on the windowsill and looked up the main street. "Let me guess," he said. "We re-create the entire village out of Legos, right?"

"No," Finkter said. "That would take too long. I wash thinking that we should wait until all the old fartsh are in bed, and Crump hash locked up the clubhoush. Then we jusht go up there to the maintenansh shed, get into to the tunnel through the air vent, and get to the clubhoush that way."

"Excuse me?" said Sir Stanford. "What tunnel?"

Oglesby cut in, holding up his hand. "I've heard about this tunnel before, Stanford, but I thought it was just an old wives' tale."

"Oh no," said Finkter, as he walked a plastic police officer up to the clubhouse steps. "I ushed to play with my shnake in it when I wash shmall. It comsh out right here, under the veranda, and it goesh all the way to Gushett Hall. It's been there for agesh. Shome old monk needed a way to get in and out of the monashtery without being sheen. I mean, it doshn't get you *into* the clubhoush, but it'll get you there without being notished."

Sir Stanford was looking at Finkter very closely.

"Really?" he said.

Finkter placed the policeman outside Uncle Dickie's office. "Yesh," he said. "And then, if shomeone had a glash cutter." Finkter stopped and looked at Mellon. "They could jusht cut a hole in the front door window pane, and open it from the inshide."

"Why would we need to get into the clubhouse?" Oglesby asked.

"I thought you wanted the clubsh?" Finkter replied.

Sir Stanford was up now, and pacing around the bar. "Do you know where the clubs are?" he said.

"Yesh," said Finkter, tapping the policeman up and down outside Uncle Dickie's office. "Right under here. My friend Fritz from Nerdlington told me hish dad worked on the conshtruction crew. It won't be eashy to get at them, but they're right there."

Flanagan couldn't sleep. He was worried about Dwilby, and Thirsty was snoring loudly on the sofa in the front room. Mills was outside with the field glasses trained on the compound, and Boon, Stanley, and Tweezer were stretched out in the spare room upstairs. He got up from the kitchen table, and checked his watch. It was just past midnight, so the boys could rest another four hours before they had to take up positions. He went outside, and let out a long low whistle.

Dwilby had soon tired of chasing the sheep, and had decided he needed something to eat. The wind was carrying a couple of different and interesting odors up from the compound, so he decided to go and investigate. Behind Shuggie's hut, he found a large ham bone, but it looked like it had been turned on a lathe. Even the marrow had been sucked from it, and he soon tired of trying to extract any nourishment. He trotted over to the remains of the bonfire, rooted out a few scraps of fatty meat, and then discovered a dead seagull, which he gnawed at for a while. Then he found a warm spot by the chimney on the leeward wall of Gregor's hut and curled up to sleep. His little stomach gave an ominous gurgle. Flanagan didn't know it, but had he been lying with Agnes and Dwilby tonight, he would be getting even less sleep.

CHAPTER FIFTEEN

Dwilby woke up shivering, and cocked his head to listen to a sound he had never heard before. The foghorn blast reverberated in the dead calm, and the only other sound that Dwilby could hear was the gentle licking of tiny waves at the shore. He stood up, stretched, and shook himself vigorously. He was hungry, and there was nothing doing around here, so he trotted down to the shoreline and began to investigate the beach. He picked his way daintily between the rocks and weed, turning up a couple of interesting smells but nothing he could swallow. A hermit crab was making its way from one pool to the next and had to endure several minutes of being sniffed, licked, scraped, and clawed along the sand, but there was nothing doing there either, so Dwilby headed on into the darkness.

Then, a little farther on, he stopped and waved his button nose in the air once more. Here was a smell that he recognized, he thought. He approached the little red car cautiously and put his front paws halfway up the driver's door. There was definitely food in there. He coiled up and sprang through the window frame, landing on the driver's seat, and hopped into the back, where there was a half-eaten bar of chocolate on the floor and the remains of a cheese sandwich wedged in the seat. It was warmer inside and also there was the familiar smell of someone he knew, so he curled up and lay down, and began to nibble at the chocolate.

Less than a mile away, over two hills and one rocky inlet, Flanagan was rousing the troops. Thirsty sat on the edge of the sofa and scratched his head, while Hammy stood at the stove, waiting for the kettle to boil once more.

"How d'ye feel, wee man?" Flanagan asked.

Thirsty looked at him, bleary-eyed, said, "It's too early to make a statement," and lay down again. "Bloody hell, Seamus, What time is it?"

"Four o'clock, and it's time to get goin', Thirsty. The Major wants ye out in front of his ball, remember?"

Thirsty swung his little legs over the edge of the sofa again, put his hands on his knees, and yawned. Hammy poured boiling water into a line of cups and stirred them, and then brought one over to Thirsty. "Coffee," he said. " It's only instant, but it'll get ye goin'."

Flanagan yelled up the stairs, and soon Stanley, Mills, and Boon joined the group around the kitchen table, and Tweezer rolled in from outside, with the field glasses around his neck. A container ship was steaming into the firth, its lights sending long streaking reflections across the coal-black water, as Thirsty got up to look out the window. "No sign of the fog you were talking about, Hammy," he said.

Hammy shook his head, as he poured Tweezer a cup of coffee. "It'll be in soon enough, don't wurry. You'll see it when the sun rises, ah can hear the foghorns already."

After eating thick slices of toast and ham, Thirsty, Mills, and Boon dressed warmly and stepped out into the darkness, each of them carrying a map and a flashlight. They made their way down the hill to the edge of the compound, where everything was eerily still. Then they split up and headed for their positions.

Stanley stood at the window with his hands in his pockets, beside Tweezer and Flanagan. "What did Uncle Dickie tell you he wanted me to do?" he asked.

Flanagan put his hand on his shoulder and patted him. "Sorry, Stanley, but the Major felt that you'd done enough already. He wants ye to stay here, an' keep an eye on Hammy." He winked, and nodded at the old man, who was outside the window, lighting his pipe. Stanley gasped. "You don't mean, I mean, the Major doesn't think that Hammy would betray us, does he?"

Flanagan pursed his lips. "Ah don't know, Stanley," he said. "But ah do know that blood's thicker than water."

The alarm buzzed, and Uncle Dickie sat up straight in bed. He took off his black silk eyeshades and, like a little boy hoping for snow, he hopped nimbly over to the window and drew the curtains back. The sky was crystal clear, and a big freighter was gliding past, leaving a veil of white foam in its wake.

"Excellent!" he said to himself, and rubbed his hands together. He ran the shower, and as he waited for the water to warm up, he did twenty deep-knee bends, twenty sit-ups, and twenty push-ups. Then he took his shaving mug and brush, soap, and a razor, jumped into the shower, and started to yodel.

A few moments later, the Maharajah put a pillow over his head and turned over, but it was no good. He was awake, and the noise from the next room was going to keep him that way. The electronic alarm clock read 4:45 A.M., as he swung his skinny brown legs over the side of the bed, and reached for his red silk night robe. Then he ran his fingers through his gray hair, pulled it into a long ponytail, and tied it back with a rubber band.

"Oooh my aching vindaloo bottom," he mumbled to himself as he opened the door to the lounge and stumbled across the carpet to Uncle Dickie's room.

Uncle Dickie stopped yodeling, and rubbed a hole in the condensation, when he heard the bathroom door open.

"Poony, old trout!"he yelled. "A cheery good morning to you!"

The Maharajah glared at him through the glass. "Oh yes," he mimicked. "I am well aware of just how cheery and good the morning is for you, but I might point out to you, that it is still the middle of the night for most people!"

"Nonsense!" cried Uncle Dickie, as he loofahed energetically between his legs, and over his shoulders. "We need to be on the road in forty-five minutes, so I suggest you get in the shower also, and scrub your old dingleberries!"

"Oh, all right, all right," the Maharajah grumbled, waving a hand at Uncle Dickie. "Just as long as you stop that bloody awful yodeling."

The Maharajah was making his way back to his room, mumbling about how people who could be cheerful at that time of the morning should be locked up somewhere, when Uncle Dickie started to whistle.

Twenty minutes later, the Maharajah was dressed in a black turban, a pair of long black baggy, silk-and-wool pants over a flowing shirt of the same material, when he went to investigate what was keeping Uncle Dickie. He was sitting on the edge of his bed, tying his shoelaces slowly and deliberately, when the Maharajah stopped in the doorway.

"What the bloody hell are you doing," he asked. "I have four feet of hair, and seventy yards of silk in my turban, and I'm ready before you?"

Uncle Dickie looked up. "Just taking a leaf from old Bobby Locke's book, Poony, you know? He did everything slowly before a big game. He dressed slowly, chewed his food slowly, even drove to the course slowly, said it was good for his rhythm. Old Bobby won five Open Championships, you know."

The Maharajah looked unimpressed. "Yes," he said. "He most probably would have won a great many more, if he hadn't been late for his bloody tee time so often."

Uncle Dickie stood up, and examined himself in the mirror. He was resplendent in a crimson silk tie, a white long-sleeved shirt, vented behind the shoulders for range of movement, a paisley Gore-Tex waistcoat with pleated houndstooth tweed plus twos, long black woolen socks with tasseled garters, and a pair of black wingtip oxfords. He twisted the tips of his mustache, and said, "Splendid!"

The Maharajah had finished his breakfast before Uncle Dickie started his. After drinking a cup of tea, he picked up his knife and fork, and slowly cut into his egg.

The Maharajah was staring at him.

"What?" he said.

"You're even swallowing slowly, aren't you? I can see you squeezing it down your throat."

Uncle Dickie smiled, and gestured with his fork. "You can

never prepare too thoroughly."

At exactly six o'clock, Uncle Dickie fired up the Bentley, and cruised majestically out of the parking lot of the Aberfeldy Palace. He slipped a CD into the dash, pulled out onto the coast road, and let the big car drift up to a steady thirty-five miles an hour. When the first few bars of "Handel's Largo" swelled from the sound system, the Maharajah let his seat back and said, "Wake me up when we get there."

Hamish had the clan lined up by the campfire and was issuing final instructions as the Bentley bounced into view. The toughened-up suspension that Mills had installed was designed for high-speed cornering and did not cope well with the mud and rocks of the McGregors' lane. By the time the car drew up outside Hamish's hut, it was plastered in muddy water all the way up to the door handles. Uncle Dickie and the Maharajah stepped out just as Hamish finished, telling the men to stay in position. Then he swaggered over to the Bentley as the white Bedford pulled up alongside, and Flanagan hopped down from the passenger seat. A few seconds later, Tweezer pushed himself across the rough surface to join them.

Hamish stood with his hands on his hips, his dark eyes glinting malevolently in the low sunlight. "And a very good morning t'you, Gussett!" he snarled. "And welcome t'the home of golf, the glorious Tay Club, where men are men, the game is played, and the sheep are still afraid!" He laughed and walked around the Bentley, letting out a low wolf whistle. "Whoa, she's a beauty, though, isn't she?" he said, looking at Uncle Dickie. "Ah don't suppose ye'd want to throw her intae the bet, would ye?"

Uncle Dickie stared at him, unblinking. "As you very well know, McGregor, there is only one thing in this pile of festering sheep droppings you call Home in which I have the slightest interest. We will compete for the Digit, over one round, match play, with the winner taking the trophy home and being regarded as the undisputed champion of the century. Is that agreed?"

Hamish was walking around the Bentley, eyeing Flanagan and Tweezer carefully.

"Och, aye, Gussett," he said dismissively, flicking a hand in his direction. "Whatever ye think ye're playin' fer here, tha's fine wi' me. Ah'm jist sayin' it's awfy nice tae have ye up here, with all yer nice things. Ye know us poor clansmen, we dinnae have these kinds of things up here." He stopped and put one bony hand on Tweezer's shoulder, and the other on Flanagan's. "You fellas," he said nastily, "would be unemployable anywhere else, wuddn't ye?" He looked over at Uncle Dickie, who was smiling curiously at Tweezer. "Is tha' not right, Gussett?" he jabbed. "Wheelie boy here wud be at a red light somewhere, wi' a wee tin cup…Aargh!"

Tweezer had reached up and grabbed Hamish's hand, and pulled him clean over his shoulder. Then he released the brake on the chair and pushed himself and the wriggling clansman over in front of Uncle Dickie, where he dropped him in the mud.

Hamish struggled to his feet and pulled down his kilt, which at one stage had been draped over his head.

"Still got a few Band-aids on down there, Hamish?" Uncle

Dickie laughed. "For your information, Wheelie boy here has a Master's degree in chemical engineering from Oxford and as you can see, he's perfectly capable of fighting his own battles!"

Hamish was flushed and furious. He glared murderously at Uncle Dickie, pointed a finger, and said sternly. "Okay, Gussett, this'll be a battle all right and we start in the Low House in ten minutes. Ye'd better hope yiv' got the stomach fer it." He marched back toward the clan, noticing that Shuggie seemed to be having difficulty controlling himself. As he stamped past, he wasn't sure, but Shuggie's cheeks appeared to be wet. He stopped, and the men shuffled about nervously, once again separating themselves from the hapless, fat clansman. "Wha's a matter, Shug?" he said suspiciously, poking him in the belly. "Did ye see something funny?"

Shuggie squirmed. "Ooh, no Hamish," he bleated, "ah just have a touch of the hay fever, tha's all."

"Aye. Very good," Hamish said, turning to the rest of the men. He hissed under his breath, "You men had better be on yer toes here today, these bastards aren't just as helpless as they look. Ah'm goin' tae change fer golf; the rest of ye get into yer positions. Gregor, get the sticks an' ah'll see ye on the tee."

The clan turned and split up as Hamish stamped back to his hut, slamming the door behind him. Uncle Dickie stood beside the Bentley with the Maharajah and watched as the men headed off over fences, up the great sand dunes, and into the hollows out of sight. He sighed and began to put on his golf shoes. "It's going to be a tough one," he said.

The Maharajah was rolling a cigarette. He paused and looked

out to sea, and said, "Well, at least we can see where we are going, old boy. There is no sign of the fog yet."

Uncle Dickie finished tying his shoelaces and stood up. He squinted across the glassy firth, into the rising sun. "Yes," he said. "Not yet."

Flanagan had the bag of Hogans out and was wiping off the rear of the car, which was caked in mud. He went to the rear door, opened it, and slid out the long leather case that held the special clubs, which he slotted, one by one, into the auxiliary bag. Then he took the auxiliary bag and strapped it tightly into the harness behind Tweezer's wheelchair. Tweezer reached over his shoulder and slipped a couple of clubs in and out, like arrows from a quiver.

"That's perfect, Seamus," he said, and began to push himself over the rough ground toward the first tee, and the distillery behind, as Flanagan hoisted the heavy bag onto his shoulder, and followed in the wide tire tracks left by Tweezer's special spiked winter wheels.

Over at the second Light House Distillery, Boon had taken up his position outside the light some hours earlier and was crouched beneath the low wall, looking through the telescopic lens of his rifle. From way up there, he had a great view of the entire golf course and the McGregors as they spread out like weevils among the hummocks and tufts. To the east he also had a clear look at a gigantic rolling blanket of clouds that was lying on the flat sea and creeping slowly toward shore.

He swept across the middle of the first hole, about a thousand yards out, and spotted the tiny figure of Thirsty, who was curled up like a rabbit just below the crest of a tufted grassy bank. A burly clansman was making his way up the other side, directly toward him. Boon pressed a little button on the cord that hung from his earpiece and whispered, "Wee man, tartan farter at twelve o'clock."

Thirsty squeezed on his switch. "I have him."

Boon watched as Angus McGregor stopped at the top of the slope to gather his breath and laughed out loud when Thirsty appeared beneath the hemline of his kilt and head-butted him viciously in the left knee. Angus clutched his bruised kneecap and hopped around for a moment, while Thirsty produced several plastic cable straps. Boon felt as if he was watching a silent movie, as Thirsty danced around Angus, staying out of the way of his lumbering swings, and darted in to kick the other knee. With a roar of surprise, Angus went down and Thirsty zipped one of the tough plastic straps around his feet and locked it. Then he bound Angus's wrists to his ankles, removed the dirk from his sock, and shoved him over the edge of the slope.

Up in the lighthouse, Boon pressed his button once more. "Very nice, wee man," he giggled, "I didn't know you were in the SAS."

"I was," said Thirsty, as he scurried off toward the cover of the next dune. "The psychopathic arsehole service!"

Hamish stood in the office of the Low House with his hand on his forehead, staring down at the prostrate figure of Stuart McGregor. He turned to Callum and Jockie, who were looking on, baffled.

"He looks like he had an argument with a double-decker

bus!" said Jockie.

"Just get him oot o' here," Hamish said angrily, waving toward the back door. "Here comes Gussett and Captain Curry."

Callum and Jockie took an armpit each and dragged Stuart off into the distillery. A few moments later, Uncle Dickie opened the door and entered, followed by the Maharajah. Hamish sat down at the desk and produced a heavy oak cask from a drawer. "Just a small traditional ceremony, Gussett," he said, opening the box and pulling out two large shot glasses. Inside the box, lying in red crushed velvet, were six ancient-looking flasks. "The original six malts of the McGregors," Hamish said. "All of them more than six hundred years old. You and I are going t'down one of each before w' tee off, and when w'get to the Light House, we're goin' tae do it again."

"How quaint," said Uncle Dickie.

"Yes, quite," said Hamish with a wicked smile. "An' if ye make it to the Last House—an' ye'd be the first to do so—we'll have one more go at it fer good luck!"

The Maharajah stepped forward and removed the first bottle. He looked at Hamish.

"May I?" he asked.

"Ooh, help yerself, Mahatma," Hamish said. "Ye know, after we're done wi' this, we cud get you a job as a cloakroom attendant, ye know? Mahatma Coat?" Hamish slapped his thigh and dabbed at his eyes with the hem of his kilt. "Oooooh, ho ho, tha's a wee beauty, isn't it? Mahatma coat!"

The Maharajah ignored him, pulled out the stopper, and ran

the bottle under his nose. "Mmmm, very nice, Mr. McGregor. Six hundred years old, you say?"

"Aye," said Hamish, "Try a wee snifter."

The Maharajah poured a good-sized measure into one of the glasses, tossed it back, swirled it for a moment, and then swallowed. Uncle Dickie looked at him anxiously.

Poonsavvy raised an eyebrow, and started to speak, but even though his lips were moving, no sound came out. With a surprised look on his face, he stopped and reached for his throat.

He shrugged his shoulders at Uncle Dickie, who produced a small bottle of brownish fluid, and waved it in front of him. The Maharajah nodded at it and gave him the thumbs up.

Hamish was enjoying himself. "Whassamatter there, Tandoori boy?" he gloated. "I thought you curry-munchers were used tae the hot stuff, or is tha' just when it's skitin' oot yer arse?"

Uncle Dickie looked out the window and saw in the distance that the Haar was approaching. "Come on, McGregor," he snapped. "Pour your firewater and let's get this done." He pulled the cork out of the bottle of Agnes Flanagan's gut primer and drained it.

"GAAAHH!" he gasped and thumped the table with his fist. He stood up and shook his jowls, shuddering and twitching violently.

The Maharajah found his voice. "Dear God, Dickie," he croaked, "I have never seen anyone drink so much of that before."

Hamish had filled the shot glasses from the first bottle and he handed one to Uncle Dickie. "Up yours!" Hamish shouted and tossed his down. He slammed the glass down hard and glared at

Uncle Dickie, who raised his, and followed suit. He gasped and gripped the edge of the table.

"Haaa!" roared Hamish, as he filled the glasses from the second flask. "This one spent a century in a sheep's bladder; ye'll love it!"

The two men continued until the last malt had been swallowed, and it was Uncle Dickie who looked less steady as they made their way to the tee. Out in the firth, a huge container ship came gliding silently toward them out of the Haar, which was now only about four hundred yards off shore. Hamish seemed to be in rare form as he signaled to Jockie, who was standing at attention over beside a large iron cannon.

"Let the match begin!" Hamish screamed at the top of his voice, bringing down his arm. Jockie lit the fuse on the cannon, took a step back, and covered his ears. There was an earth-shattering explosion, and Jockie and the cannon were enveloped in a huge cloud of smoke. Then there was silence for a few seconds.

As the smoke drifted away, Hamish staggered around with his hands over his ears. He turned to look at Jockie, who was lying on his back behind the cannon, his elderly privates dangling over his left thigh. He clambered slowly to his feet, and pulled his kilt down.

"Wha' in the name o' God did ye put in that thing, Jockie?" Hamish said.

Jockie was staring out to sea. He pointed at the ship and turned to Hamish. "One of those," he said in a very small voice. Hamish looked, just in time to see a heavy black cannonball collide with the white sheet metal of the ship's bridge. A second or two later, a resounding "Crump," floated back across the water to them, followed by a "Clang" as the cannonball fell to the deck. Hamish looked at Jockie, who was staring at his Wellington boots.

"You mean tae tell me, tha' ye put a live charge in there wi' a fifty-pound cannonball, and aimed it at a Panamanian container ship?" Hamish asked incredulously.

Jockie shifted nervously from one foot to the other, and pointed at the ship again. "Actually," he stammered, "It was a double charge, an' if ye look closely Hamish, ah think that ship's maybe Russian. Ah think that's a sickle yer man on the bridge is wavin' at us."

Hamish stared skyward, trembling with rage, but the matter at hand quickly came back to him. "Brilliant," he said to himself, drawing a huge breath. "We just declared war on the Soviet Union."

He turned to Uncle Dickie, who was leaning on his driver and observing with amusement.

"Eh, Hamish," Jockie said nervously. "If ye remember correctly, the Soviet Union is no longer an actual country, ye know, since the collapse of communism an' all…"

Hamish took another deep breath, exhaled slowly, and said quietly, "Jockie, if you don't shut yer pie hole right now, ah'm goin' tae personally insert tha' cannon up your arse, an' light the fuse. Okay?" He spun on his heel and pointed a gnarly finger at Uncle Dickie.

"Right, Gussett," he snapped, "Tee it up an' hit it, ye old

fart."

Uncle Dickie bent over to tee up his ball, and had to put one hand on the ground to steady himself. He set up carefully, waggled, and hit a heely cut down the left, about two hundred yards out. He staggered over to Flanagan, who said, "Good shot, sir. Don't you worry, me an' Tweezer'll get ye 'round here, no problem."

Hamish had already addressed his ball and took a mighty flailing swing at it, sending it rocketing out toward the shore and drawing back to the right edge of the fairway. It carried forty yards past Uncle Dickie's ball, and rolled another twenty. Hamish let out a whoop of delight, threw his driver to Gregor, and marched off up the fairway.

Over the hill, the noise of the explosion had awakened Dwilby with a start. He had become accustomed to the gentle throbbing of the foghorns, but this one was a shock. He hopped out of the mini, shook himself, and started back up the beach.

Uncle Dickie, Flanagan, and Tweezer followed Hamish, while the Maharajah ambled slowly down the edge of the beach. "What is the par of this hole, Flanagan?" asked Uncle Dickie.

"It's a par-twenty-three," said Flanagan.

"Hey, McGregor!" Uncle Dickie shouted. "If I make a twenty-two here, would that be a birdie?"

McGregor turned to look back at the strange-looking group that was trailing him and yelled, "Ah'll make you a deal, old man. If you can make one birdie on this golf course today, ye can have the first distillery!"

"Oh, Dickie," called the Maharajah from the beach. "Do

play well, old boy. That stuff gives a person an incredible buzz!"

Uncle Dickie waved and loosened the knot in his tie. "All right then, Flanagan. Where do we need to be?"

Flanagan pointed straight down the coast. "We need to keep it to the left down here, sir, as the sea cuts in a little more than you think. Two more good hits and we can carry the first dunes with our fourth. If you mishit either of them, we'll have to lay up."

Uncle Dickie hit his next two fairway metal woods solidly, but Hamish had already carried the Dunes in three huge shots and was out of sight from the old man as he hit his fourth. He was not out of Boon's sight, though, and as Uncle Dickie's ball bounded past Hamish, the marksman watched closely as the McGregor Chieftain made a hand signal. Out of the low scrubby gorse bushes some eighty yards ahead, a small kilted figure came scurrying out. Boon lifted his nose from the gunsight and sniffed the wind. It was about a six-hundred-yard shot, he figured. Then he drew a bead with the silenced .22, about a foot short of Uncle Dickie's ball. The little slug got there before anyone heard the low crack of the rifle. Finlay McGregor's skinny fingers were just inches from snatching the ball, when the earth below his face was torn up, sending a stinging sheet of sand into his eyes. He yelped and jumped back, and stumbled back into the gorse, clutching his face.

"Shite!" Hamish hissed, stamping his foot and scanning the surrounding dunes. "Gregor, what the hell happened?"

Gregor looked just as confused, as Uncle Dickie came march-

ing over the hill, followed by Flanagan, who was pushing Tweezer.

"Not exactly wheelchair accessible," Hamish said sarcastically, as the little group joined Gregor and him. Hamish snatched a metal wood from the bag and took another mighty swing, but this time the ball curved violently to the right, and came to rest on the beach.

"Oooh!" said Uncle Dickie, "I had no idea the hole went in that direction. I thought we had to keep it out of the sea!"

Hamish was still glaring all around him as he marched off toward the shore, where the Maharajah was already waving at him. "Oh, yes, Mr. McGregor!" he shouted. "You are going to love this one! It's right under a most beautiful piece of driftwood, that looks exactly like an elephant's willie!"

Uncle Dickie noticed a thin tear in the tight fescue, just short of his ball. He grinned at Flanagan as he set up over another metalwood. "Looks like Boon can still shoot the balls off a blowfly from a mile away," he said, as he hit an elegant high draw that carried about 220 yards, landed on a downslope, and took a hard bounce forward. The Maharajah was hanging around Hamish and Gregor, and they were none too pleased. Hamish took three mighty whacks at his ball and broke two clubs on the driftwood before he managed to get back to the fairway.

By the time the first green had come into view, Hamish had made up the ground on Uncle Dickie again and soon they were under the shadow of the Light House Distillery, about sixty yards short of the green. Uncle Dickie and Hamish had played twenty-three shots each, as Hamish played a low 6-iron bump-and-run, which curled up about twelve feet behind the hole. The flagstick was placed on the front edge of the green, just over a little mound, and Hamish had judged his approach perfectly. Uncle Dickie turned to Tweezer. "Give me the Bungley backup wedge there, dear boy," he said. "This calls for a little action."

Tweezer unsheathed an old hickory short iron with a strange-looking toe and handed it to Uncle Dickie, who pulled a small key from his pocket. Hamish looked on curiously, as Uncle Dickie inserted the key into the toe of the club, and twisted it several times. With each twist, the grooves on the face of the wedge crept upward, until Uncle Dickie felt he had the right tension. He set up and hooked his index finger through a brass ring on the underside of the grip. Then, with the ball back in his stance, he made a short positive swing, hitting down and taking a deep divot after the ball. As the clubhead made contact with the ball, he tugged on the ring and released the spring, bringing the grooves down the face, sending out a low, skidding shot, which took a hard hop at the front of the green and skipped to the back edge. Hamish let out a shout of triumph, but his joy soon turned to horror, as the ball suddenly zipped violently backward, and sped smoothly back down the green, finishing within inches of the cup.

"Shite!" Hamish roared.

The Maharajah applauded politely from the edge of the green. "My heavens, McGregor," he chortled. "Did you ever see one like that? Why, it came back like an elephant's foreskin!"

The Haar was lurking menacingly just offshore, and a gentle

breeze was pushing it slowly landward. It seemed unlikely that Uncle Dickie would see where he was going on the next, so he, Flanagan, and Tweezer had their fingers crossed, as Hamish addressed his putt for a half.

Hamish took up a curiously knock-kneed stance, and hunched over the ball with an old Ping Anser. After wiggling around for what seemed like an eternity, he jabbed at it, and the ball glanced in and out of the right half of the hole. He flinched and screamed, "BOLLOCKS!" at the top of his voice.

CHAPTER SIXTEEN

"One up Gussett, ye jammy old fart," Hamish growled, as he and Uncle Dickie walked to the Light House. "Ah have t'be honest, ah thought it wud pretty much be over by now, but it definitely will be after this!" He opened the door at the bottom of the tower and slipped inside, returning some moments later with another wooden casket. Two glasses were produced and another array of antique flasks.

Uncle Dickie had started to feel a little better toward the end of the first hole, but after downing the next six shots, he was hammered, to say the least. McGregor was also feeling the effect of the fiery liquor but was younger and stronger, and after his first dozen strokes on the second hole, a brutally long par-30, he was a long way ahead of the older man. The Haar had closed in, making local knowledge a huge advantage. Uncle Dickie, who had stuck to the right side of the fairway, found himself in a strangely barren area, littered with seaweed and shells, when Hamish appeared out of the mist, standing about fifteen feet above him on a grassy bank.

"Yer in the Nostril, Gussett," he laughed.

Uncle Dickie ignored him and bent down to examine his lie. A small pebble rested against the side of his ball, right on the spot where his club would make contact. It looked as if the ball might shoot off in any direction if Uncle Dickie tried to hit it with any normal golf club, but the old man seemed unperturbed as he called over to Tweezer, "The Deliverer, if you please, my boy."

Tweezer rolled over with the auxiliary clubs, and sorted through the leather sleeves until he found the one he wanted. He withdrew a hickory-shafted iron with a strange toothed head. Uncle Dickie took it from him and examined it, smiling.

"A reverse rake," he called over to Hamish, who was watching with interest. "Just the ticket to catch the ball and miss the impediment that lies against it." Hamish looked unimpressed and seemed more interested in the waves that splashed gently against the rocks behind.

"Aye, whatever, Gussett," he said impatiently. "Just hit the bloody ball."

Uncle Dickie took aim at the back of the ball, carefully placing the head of the club so that the little stone matched up with one of the wide gaps in the face, and made his swing. The ball shot straight and true, back to the middle of the fairway, and Uncle Dickie was posing on his follow-through, when suddenly, there was a loud, "PLOOOF" to his right, and he was struck by an icy jet of sea water, weed, and pebbles that knocked him to the ground.

Hamish was falling around, laughing. "Oooh, ho ho, hee hee," he said. "There's a blowhole in the rocks over there. We call it the Nostril because it'll cover ye in tha' green sea-snot if yer no' careful."

Uncle Dickie picked himself up, and removed a strand of kelp from his head. "Very clever, McGregor," he said. "Pity you need the sideshows to make this place interesting."

Mills and Thirsty watched through the thickening mist, from under a low bank at the edge of the shore. Between them, they had already disabled and hogtied several of the McGregors, and Thirsty had called for Boon to come down from the Light, as it was impossible to see anything from ground level, never mind up there. Hamish slowly increased his lead and was hitting only one shot every few minutes or so, as he waited for Uncle Dickie to catch up. He had reached the edge of the second green in twenty-six shots to Uncle Dickie's thirty, when the old man and his caddies finally got there.

"Aha, Gussett!" he said cheerfully. "Awfully nice of ye t'join us. Ah thought tha' maybe ye had died back there."

Uncle Dickie walked unsteadily over to his ball, and squinted at Flanagan, who was tending the flagstick. "Bloody hell, Flanagan," he hissed. "I can see two holes!" Uncle Dickie was swaying around and appeared to be using the putter as a crutch. Flanagan was worried he might fall over at any minute. "Just aim it at the biggest one, sir," he said.

Uncle Dickie flicked at the ball, which wobbled down the slope to the hole, stopped momentarily on the front edge, and then lurched in. Flanagan let out a yell and danced around the hole, as the Maharajah politely applauded from the edge of the green.

But the second hole had been lost.

Hamish hunched over his putter and rolled the ball up stone dead. "Tha'll be twenty-eight. How duz tha' tickle yer fancy?"

Hamish turned his back, and set off up the stone steps to the Last House. "Och, aye, very good, Gussett, so now we're all square," he said. "But yiv got six more wee drams tae deal with, and ye don't know where yer goin'. Follow me."

They climbed the steps slowly, and Uncle Dickie tried not to look down. Flanagan was sober but none too steady on his feet either, as the beach below slowly disappeared into the fog. Uncle Dickie was out of breath, and Hamish was waiting for him with a glass in each hand when he got to the top and stepped on to the last tee, high up on the bluff. Down below, he could see Tweezer, the Maharajah, Mills, and Boon, disappearing into the slow, creeping mist, as they made their way along the narrow path that led to the landing area.

"Aye," said Hamish. "The Haar looks nice from up here, but we'll be back doon amongst it in a minute. Here," he said, shoving the glass under Uncle Dickie's nose. "Chin-chin, old boy!"

As Uncle Dickie threw back his shot, Hamish surreptitiously tossed his own over his shoulder and wiped his mouth. Flanagan was holding Uncle Dickie up now and was terrified that the old man would lose his footing and plunge to his death on the rocks below. Hamish handed him another glass, and Flanagan protested. "Aw, there's no way, sir," he said. "Ah can't let you drink any more, it's goin' ta kill ye!"

"Maybe!" shouted Hamish, who had just tossed another one over the side. "Just like Sir Basil Strangely-Smallpiece!"

Uncle Dickie suddenly straightened up, and with a murderous gleam in his eyes, staggered over in front of Hamish.

"Oooh," said Hamish. "It's alive!"

Uncle Dickie snatched the glass from him.

"Yes, I am, McGregor," Uncle Dickie slurred, taking a lurching step backward and then forward once more. He stabbed a finger into Hamish's chest and tossed the shot back. "And you are going to wish that you had never uttered the name of that saintly man." He nodded over at the box. "Now drink up, you smelly Caledonian cretin! And play golf!"

Hamish had to drink the final three shots, as Uncle Dickie was still in his face, and he didn't realize how smashed he was until he staggered forward a little as he was teeing up his ball. He shook his head and settled himself. Then he took a mighty slash. The ball shot straight down the middle and disappeared into the enveloping mist below. He chuckled as, unsteadily, he handed the driver back to Gregor. "Tha's the hard bit on this hole, Gussett."

Uncle Dickie was tremendously inebriated, but the mention of Sir Basil had hardened his resolve. He teed his ball up higher than normal, swung his Hogan oversize driver as hard as he could, and felt sweet contact, as the ball shot off high and straight and fell into the mist below.

Hamish harrumphed as he made his way off the tee. "Yer in the dark again, Gussett," he said malevolently.

Back on the beach, Dwilby was trotting quickly in the direction of a familiar sound. He had got to the stage where he was starting to miss the human company for which he usually showed such disdain, mainly because he was starving. The speed slot in the toe of Uncle Dickie's Hogan driver caused the club to make a high-frequency sound as the clubhead rushed toward the ball. It was inaudible to humans, but Dwilby knew it instantly from his many rounds with Flanagan and Uncle Dickie at the Wood, after which he usually got fed, so he was making a beeline for it.

Down on the fairway, Thirsty, Mills, Boon, and Tweezer

heard the balls land, and the Maharajah walked out to identify them. "Who is playing the one with the two black stripes upon it?" he called back out of the gloom.

"That would be McGregor," yelled Thirsty, who had been splashed as he walked underneath the last tee, with something that smelled remarkably like whisky. Somebody had been throwing perfectly good whisky away and that was just the sort of thing that made Thirsty very, very angry. Which he was anyway, because he was stone cold sober. "The Major plays a Spalding!" he shouted.

Tweezer sat by Uncle Dickie's Top-Flite and waited for Flanagan and Uncle Dickie to appear out of the mist. Hamish marched by first, weaving a drunken path across the fairway. His ball was only about forty yards in front of Uncle Dickie's, but by the time he got there, he and Gregor were completely hidden by the fog. Uncle Dickie suddenly emerged from the steam and took Tweezer by the shoulder. "Listen, my boy," he said in a conspiratorial stage whisper. "I want you to prepare the bangstick for me, and I need it to be set for around a thousand yards."

Tweezer looked back into Uncle Dickie's glazed eyes, and stammered, "B-b-b-ut, sir! That's far too big a charge! You could seriously injure, or even kill yourself, if you try to hit it that far."

Uncle Dickie reached into the Hogan bag on Flanagan's shoulder and struggled to pull a welder's mask from the side compartment. He slipped on the headband, pulled down the visor, and got down in front of Tweezer's face.

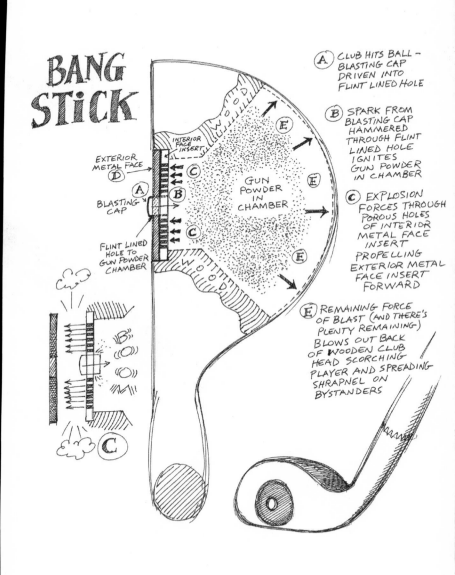

BANG STiCK

(A) CLUB HITS BALL –
BLASTING CAP
DRIVEN INTO
FLINT LINED HOLE

(B) SPARK FROM
BLASTING CAP
HAMMERED
THROUGH FLINT
LINED HOLE
IGNITES
GUN POWDER
IN CHAMBER

(C) EXPLOSION
FORCES THROUGH
POROUS HOLES
OF INTERIOR
METAL FACE
INSERT
PROPELLING
EXTERIOR METAL
FACE INSERT
FORWARD

(E) REMAINING FORCE
OF BLAST (AND THERE'S
PLENTY REMAINING)
BLOWS OUT BACK
OF WOODEN CLUB
HEAD SCORCHING
PLAYER AND SPREADING
SHRAPNEL ON
BYSTANDERS

EXTERIOR
METAL FACE
(D)

BLASTING
CAP

FLINT LINED
HOLE TO
GUN POWDER
CHAMBER

INTERIOR
FACE
INSERT

WOOD

GUN
POWDER
IN
CHAMBER

WOOD

The Bangstick or "Explode-O-Matic Driver" (Hollingsworth, Merrill W. *Santa Barbara, California. 1910*).

The patent for this club was issued on November 22, 1910; and, to the author's knowledge, the only example made was destroyed in the incident described in this book. The "Explode-O-Matic" had a wooden head with a slotted metal insert that, when removed, revealed a triangular powder chamber. A drilled metal plate, complete with built-in blast cap, was fitted into the slot in the insert; in effect, the ball then became the firing pin. Upon impact, the two plates compressed, firing the cap and igniting the charge and, apparently, anything else within a yard or two. The insert was then propelled forward very quickly indeed, and would never be found. The Bangstick was worth a fortune and, according to Uncle Dickie, "worth every blasted penny."

"I thought of that."

Flanagan looked over. "Bloody hell!" he said. "I wondered why this friggin' bag was so heavy!"

Uncle Dickie hit his ball another nine times, with Tweezer rolling along beside him, working away at the strange hickory-shafted club. Hamish was nowhere to be seen, but the Maharajah had been glued to Gregor and him and he had played eleven on the final par-19 hole, when there was a sudden change in the weather. The gentle breeze had changed direction, and as quickly as the Haar had made landfall, it now began to shrink back toward the shore.

Hammy and Stanley were up in the farmhouse, looking down at the mist. Stanley had been pacing around nervously ever since he had lost sight of Uncle Dickie on the last hole.

"There she goes!" said Hammy.

"What?" Stanley blurted out, as he rushed over to the window.

"The tide," said Hammy. "It just turned and changed the wind. The fog'll be gone in a minute."

Sure enough, as Stanley watched, the last hole began to reappear. "Come on, Hammy," Stanley said. "Let's get down there!"

Hamish and Gregor stood on the edge of the great dune, about three hundred yards short of the final green. "Where the friggin' hell are they?" said Hamish.

Gregor looked back into the thinning mist. "Ah think ah can see somebody all the way back there," he said, as a small huddle of people, about a par-5's distance back, slowly materialized into focus. Hamish squinted. "Oooh, aye," he said cheerfully. "He's miles back. Tha' should do it, Gregor!"

Back down the fairway, Flanagan said, "Inside a thousand yards, sir."

Tweezer examined the bangstick one last time. He had dropped a blast cap, and packed a quarter ounce of black powder into the chamber behind the insert of the ancient wooden club and then packed it tight with wadding. He handed it over to Uncle Dickie.

"Sir," he said. 'I'm begging you, don't hit it. It's so old, and it's never been hit before. God knows how the charge will behave."

Uncle Dickie took the club and waggled it. "Tweezer," he said. "In 1911, in Santa Barbara, California, Mr. Merrill W. Hollingsworth made this golf club, specifically for this moment. It is the only club of its kind in existence. You can say that you were here to see it operate."

He pulled the welder's mask down with a clang, and his voice was muffled as he said, "But you don't need to be quite so close, go on, get back. You too, Flanagan."

Flanagan and Tweezer moved all the way back to the edge of the beach and watched as Uncle Dickie addressed the ball.

Back up the fairway, Hamish was scratching his head, and wondering what was going on, when he saw a flash of light and, a second or so later, heard a thunderous roar. Uncle Dickie disappeared in a cloud of smoke, into which Flanagan ran headlong. Flanagan coughed and spluttered, as he felt around in the thick, gray smoke, and eventually he found Uncle

Dickie lying flat on his back. His clothes were scorched and torn, and a thin splinter of hickory was lodged in his right thigh.

"Fuck me, Gregor," said Hamish. "He blew himself up!"

Just then Hamish heard a high-pitched whistling noise, as Uncle Dickie's ball screamed overhead, and landed one hundred yards further on up the fairway. It took an enormous bounce, and ran on another fifty.

"Shite!" Hamish shrieked, and turned to look down the fairway. Uncle Dickie was limping out of the cloud of smoke, helped by Flanagan. High above his head, he was holding an old, burned leather grip, with a few charred splinters sticking out of it.

"How many has he played?" Hamish yelled at Gregor, suddenly panic-stricken.

Gregor shrugged his shoulders.

The Maharajah chipped in from a little way up the hill, "I believe that would be twelve, and you are about to hit your thirteeth, Mr. McGregor!"

"Where'd it go?" Uncle Dickie coughed, as Flanagan slapped him on the back.

"It went like a bullet, about a mile that way!" Flanagan pointed, jumping up and down with excitement.

Tweezer rolled in excitedly holding his right hand over his earpiece. "Boon says it's about a hundred and twenty yards short of the green, sir!" he said.

Uncle Dickie pulled off the mask and handed it back to Flanagan. "Right, then," he said. "Let's go finish this off, shall we?"

Hamish was muttering to himself as he set up over his thirteenth shot. "Exploding golf clubs, my arse!" He took a huge swipe with his metal 3-wood and connected sweetly. His ball sailed past Uncle Dickie's and rolled up to within a few yards of the green, and, as he handed the club back to Gregor, he lifted up the front of his kilt to expose himself to the Maharajah. "What d'ye think aboot tha', ye turbaned turd-puncher?" he hooted derisively.

The Maharajah screwed up his eyes and said, "My dear fellow, I have tremendous eyesight, but I still can't see the objects which you are asking me to describe. Ask me again when the weather gets a little warmer."

Uncle Dickie looked at Flanagan, who already had the pitching wedge in his hand. He gave it to Uncle Dickie, who was unsteady on his feet and looked as if he was ready to fall over.

"Are you all right, sir?" he asked.

Uncle Dickie mustered a last smile, and replied, "I'm still fighting, Seamus, my dear friend. I'm still fighting."

It was the first time in Flanagan's life that the old man had called him Seamus. He was not a religious man, but right then and there, Seamus Flanagan prayed that Almighty God would grant him one wish; that his Uncle Dickie would hit it close to the hole, and then sink the putt.

"Amen," Seamus said to himself, as Uncle Dickie lurched back with the club and cold topped the ball into a large embedded boulder about ten feet in front of where they stood.

Nobody saw where the ball went, as it streaked two hundred feet into the air and spun wildly off to the left. Hamish, who was standing on a flat rock forty yards short of the green, let out a primal scream of victory, as he saw Uncle Dickie collapse face first onto the fairway.

Flanagan looked heavenward and shook his fist. "Thank you very bloody much!" he yelled.

Then the ball landed on the rock in between Hamish's feet and shot upward with such force that, with a stinging smack, it wedged itself firmly between his buttocks. Hamish let out a short, high-pitched shriek of pain and surprise.

Gregor looked at him curiously. "You okay, big lad?" he said.

Hamish was cringing, and obviously in great pain. "Gregor," he squeaked.

"Wha'?"

"What d'ye call that wee piece of skin between yer arsehole an' yer bollocks?"

Gregor scratched his head. "Ah dunno, Hamish, why wud ye ask?"

Hamish looked at his younger brother with an expression that was somewhere between shock and agony. "Because that's where Gussett's ball is."

Gregor looked down at Hamish's knees, which appeared to be nailed together, and then down the fairway, where all the caddies, including Stanley, had rushed over to tend to Uncle Dickie.

"Hamish," he said out of the corner of his mouth, "did anyone else see where the ball went?"

"No, ah dinnae think so," Hamish whimpered.

"Brilliant," said Gregor. "Then as far as they know," he said, pointing at Uncle Dickie, who was on Tweezer's lap and being wheeled toward the green, "the ball is lost! All ye have t' do is finish the hole, an' keep yer arse shut. Whatever ye do, don't let him know where it is, or he might try to play it!"

"Ooh," Hamish said, looking at his brother with a pitiful expression. "Tha' wouldnae be good."

"Off ye go," whispered Gregor, "Just keep clenchin'."

Hamish hobbled knock-kneed down to his ball and scuttled it along the ground and onto the front of the green with his putter. Then he slowly made his way up and scraped another putt off, rolling the ball up to two feet, and while Gregor held the flag, he tapped it in. Behind the green, those members of the clan who had avoided the embrace of Thirsty and Mills, let out a great cheer, as Gregor said quietly to Hamish, "Why don't ye let me pick it out of the hole for ye?"

"Which hole?" Hamish said with a weak smile.

Uncle Dickie clambered out of Tweezer's lap, and limped over to the flagstick to extend his hand. "Well played, McGregor," he said, holding up his scorched chin. "The better man won the match, and I salute you."

Hamish was reaching for Uncle Dickie's hand, when Dwilby shot out of the dunes behind and skidded to a halt beneath the pleats of his kilt. Upon seeing Flanagan and Uncle Dickie, the little dog let out a joyful yelp.

"Aaaargh!" Hamish shrieked once more, lifting up his right

knee as Dwilby brushed against his leg. With a soft plop, Uncle Dickie's ball fell out, glanced off Dwilby's back, and rolled to within inches of the hole.

"Ooh, I say," Uncle Dickie said, looking at Hamish's horrified expression.

"Original rules, old boy, play the ball as it lies, and the course as you find it, eh?"

Hamish looked at the dog, then the ball, and then at Gregor, who shrugged his shoulders. His mouth hung open, but no sound emerged, as Uncle Dickie said, "Seamus, bring me the putter, if you would be so kind!"

CHAPTER SEVENTEEN

Uncle Dickie was drunk, scorched, injured, and unsteady on his feet, but he still managed easily to tap the ball into the hole. The match was over, and Flanagan, who, seconds before had been cursing the Almighty, was now dancing with joy and silently begging forgiveness.

Hamish was also drunk, and it looked as if he was not about to be the gracious loser that Uncle Dickie had been. He glared over at the remnants of the clan and snapped his fingers. "Callum!" he barked. "Give Gussett the finger again."

Callum lumbered over onto the green and reluctantly handed the old wooden box to Uncle Dickie, who was being held upright by Flanagan and Boon. The Maharajah applauded politely once more from the side of the green, as Uncle Dickie accepted the Digit and once more offered his hand to Hamish. Hamish looked at the blackened hand with its cuts and scrapes, and growled, "Yer no' out of here yet, Gussett, an' I'll no' be shakin' anythin' of yours, except maybe yer throat."

Uncle Dickie pulled himself loose from Flanagan and Boon, and straightened up. "McGregor, old boy," he said. "I really think you would be most unwise to do anything other than accept defeat gracefully. I have my men around me, and as you have seen, they are more than a match for yours." Uncle Dickie turned to face Flanagan, Mills, Boon, and Stanley, who was standing behind Tweezer. "Where's Thirsty?" he asked.

Flanagan stepped forward. "Er, sir," he began, making eye movements over his shoulder toward the Low House.

"Whereabouts unknown, sir."

"Hmm," said Uncle Dickie. "Well, no doubt he'll show up. It's time we were off."

Hamish was breathing deeply as he watched them make their way off the green and toward the big car. "Gregor!" he hissed out of the side of his mouth. "Get the lads together aroon' tha' car right noo!"

Gregor dropped the bag of clubs and went to muster the remaining men, and Hamish set off slowly behind Uncle Dickie and the boys.

Thirsty was in the Low House, putting together a care package for the road. It had taken a superhuman effort to resist topping up right away, but he knew that Uncle Dickie had to give the word first. He had found a very interesting old wooden cask with six old bottles in it, and was in the process of hoisting it to his shoulder when, through the window, he noticed Uncle Dickie and the boys at the Bentley, and that the McGregors were surrounding them. He settled the case on his shoulder and marched out.

Tweezer had just put the antique clubs in the trunk of the car when the commotion started.

Hamish stood, with his arms folded across his chest. "Now you boys don't honestly think tha' we're just goin' tae stand here and wave cheerio, do ye?" he said malevolently.

The Maharajah stood at the front of the Bentley, rolling himself another cigarette. "McGregor," he said casually. "It seems to me that many times in the last few days, it has escaped your attention that you are surrounded by morons here." He pointed at the clansmen around the car. Jockie, Callum, a heavily bandaged Stuart, Gregor, and Shuggie, all stood looking murderously back at him.

"Ye know, Captain Krishna," Hamish said, "For a fella tha' hasnae even got his fingernails dirty here, you're full of all kinds of crap."

Hamish smiled wolfishly and curled a finger toward himself. "How aboot ye come over here an put yer poxy wee brown hands up?"

The Maharajah laughed. "Oh, McGregor, you are a funny fellow also. You see, there is absolutely no need for me to do such a thing, as I have my friends here to look after me. I'm a pacifist at heart, you know? Like Gandhi."

Uncle Dickie stepped unsteadily forward. "McGregor," he said gravely. "I must warn you that any attempt you might make to either prevent us from leaving or take what is ours, will be met with the sternest resistance. For me, the battle is over. If you wish to fight again, the responsibility will lie upon your own head."

Hamish nodded to Callum and Gregor, who immediately tipped Tweezer out of his chair, and pounced on Mills and Boon. Jockie and Stuart piled on top, as Hamish grabbed Uncle Dickie around the throat, and pulled a razor-sharp dirk from his sock. He held it to Uncle Dickie's ear and screamed, "All right, all of ye stop, an' listen tae me!" Flanagan and Stanley had leapt forward to help Uncle Dickie, but stopped in their tracks, when they saw the flash of the blade.

Hamish was leering, with his huge beard scraping the side of

Uncle Dickie's face. His whisky-sodden breath was hot in the old man's nostrils as he whispered, "All right then, Uncle Dickie, let's give a few orders here, shall we? Ah want all of yer men inside the hut here, an' the keys to the jalopy. Okay?"

Uncle Dickie gasped as Hamish tightened his grip. "Do as he says, boys," he wheezed, as Hamish turned him around and used him as a shield, as Boon, Mills, Flanagan, and Stanley were led into the hut. Shuggie slammed the door, slid the bolt across, and stood with his arms folded in front of it. Tweezer pulled himself into a sitting position against the wall and could only watch as Callum, Stuart, Jockie, and Gregor started to slowly encircle the Bentley and creep closer to the Maharajah, who was backing up and fumbling in his pocket.

"The keys, curry boy," Hamish growled.

"Oh, I know they are in here somewhere," muttered the Maharajah. "Just hold on a moment." Then he popped something into his mouth, quickly drew a slim pipe from his pocket, and the four approaching clansmen heard a small, "Pliff!" as a red speck appeared in the center of Hamish's forehead.

Hamish looked vaguely surprised at first, then his eyes crossed and he went limp. His arms fell off Uncle Dickie and, slowly, with a look of astonishment on his face, he crumpled into a heap in the mud.

Uncle Dickie straightened his collar. "Good shot, old boy!" he said. "What the devil is that stuff?"

The Maharajah had popped another pellet into his mouth, and Gregor was the next to look stunned, as a bright red blotch appeared on the side of his neck. Callum came charging at him with his hands in the air, but sailed past and ran head-first into the wall of Hamish's hut, with a small red dot on his nose. But Stuart and Jockie grabbed the Maharajah before he could get another shot off.

"Punjabi Hemp Toad saliva," the Maharajah said, as they dragged him over to the wall. "It renders its recipient unconscious within five seconds, and has no aftereffects other than the occasional case where the eyeballs swell up and burst." He looked at Stuart and Jockie. "Would you chaps like to try it?"

Stuart and Jockie didn't have time to answer, as Thirsty had arrived. He set the cask down carefully beside the Bentley and saluted Uncle Dickie. "Sorry I'm a wee bit late, sir," he said. "But I thought we might need a bit of sustenance on the way home." He pulled Tweezer's chair over, and helped him up into it. "Did I miss anything?"

"Yes, actually you did," said Uncle Dickie. "McGregor had a knife to my throat, Shuggie here locked up the rest of the boys in the hut, and these two have captured the Maharajah."

Thirsty looked at Stuart and Jockie, but turned to Shuggie first. "You did what?" he said.

Shuggie, who had been careful to keep out of the way for the last few minutes, looked at the cask on the ground with horror and said, "Ye cannae take tha'. Tha's the six-hundred-year-old stuff. Hamish'll go berserk!"

"I've a feeling that Hamish will go berserk anyway, Shuggie," said Uncle Dickie. "And by the look on Thirsty's face, you'd better stand aside."

Shuggie looked down at Thirsty, who was standing defiantly

in front of him with his hands on his hips. Inside the hut, Flanagan and the boys had their faces pressed against the window.

Shuggie looked confused. "Stand aside fer this wee man here?" he giggled. "Ah've got a better idea, Mr. Gussett. Why don't ah just turn around an' fart at him, an' you can go an' pick him oot of the North Sea!"

Stuart McGregor, who had been holding the Maharajah with Jockie, suddenly realized where he had seen Thirsty's nasty little face before, and was about to warn Shuggie to be careful, just as Thirsty's tiny right foot rocketed into Shuggie's groin. It was a blow that would have started and ended most fights, but the enormous amount of cellulite at the top of Shuggie's thighs acted like an airbag and trapped Thirsty's foot short of its target for long enough to allow Shuggie to get a grip on Thirsty's pants.

"Oooh, yer a fast one okay, wee fella, but yer Uncle Shug has a bit of a weight advantage!" Shuggie grinned, as he viciously tore one leg of Thirsty's pants off, down to the ankle.

As Shuggie and Thirsty became entangled, Hamish was slowly regaining consciousness. He grasped the back fender of the Bentley, and pulled himself into a sitting position. Then, as it became evident Shuggie was gaining a fatal advantage, Hamish heaved himself upright, reached into the trunk of the Bentley, and grabbed as many of the slim leather cases as he could fit under his arm. Unnoticed, he staggered around the side of the hut, and made his escape.

Thirsty hopped around and rained punches into Shuggie's sides and stomach, but the big man's padding absorbed them all, and Uncle Dickie, the Maharajah, and the boys in the hut looked on in horror as Shuggie slowly bent Thirsty in half, and lay down on top of him. After a few moments, it looked like it was all over when Thirsty's legs and arms stopped twitching. Then suddenly, from inside the giant pile of blubber and humanity, there came a bloodcurdling scream, the like of which none of them had ever heard, and Shuggie suddenly flew through the air. With a sickening, "Thunk," he hit the stone wall of the hut with his giant forehead and rolled off down the muddy slope into an unconscious mound of lard.

Stuart and Jockie looked at one another in horror. They both let go of the Maharajah, then quickly sidled around the hut, and away from the scene. Uncle Dickie and the Maharajah tended to the exhausted Thirsty, as Tweezer let the boys out of the hut. They were jubilant, and as Uncle Dickie poured some of the McGregor malt over Thirsty's lips, Flanagan asked him, "Thirsty, tha' was unbelievable! How did ye get him off ye?"

Thirsty wiped his mouth and sat up. "Well," he said. "I must admit, I thought I was a goner when he folded me in two, and got his weight on me, you know? But then I saw it, just hangin' there in front of me."

"Saw what?" said Flanagan.

"A great big hairy dick," Thirsty explained. "So there was nothin' else I could do, I just sunk my teeth into it!"

"Ooooh!" everyone winced, and Stanley doubled up at the thought of such a thing.

"Yes," Thirsty continued. "It's amazing the surge of strength you get, when you bite your own dick!"*

Uncle Dickie clapped his hands. "Splendid!" he said. "Now everybody, follow me, it's back to the Aberfeldy Palace to get cleaned up, and perhaps a little celebration!"

Back in the Trossachs Suite, Uncle Dickie uncorked one of the bottles of 1821 Château Yquem and handed it to Thirsty. Then he opened another one and poured everyone a glass. Dwilby sat on a velvet throw pillow in the corner, chewing on a large T-bone steak.

"My friends," Uncle Dickie began. "Thank you for being with me, today and always. Your company is my greatest pleasure, your friendship, loyalty, and devotion to duty, my greatest treasure. God bless you all, and cheers!"

Stanley said, "Cheers," weakly, took a small sip, and went over to stand by the window by himself. He fought back the wave, but it was no good. He squeezed his eyelids shut, but a small tear escaped, and tumbled down the side of his nose. The boys were in great form behind him, singing and roaring with laughter, but Stanley Beamish was struggling with his conscience.

Uncle Dickie noticed him standing alone, and joined him at the window. He slipped an arm around his neck and said quietly, "You know, Stanley, I'm so very proud of you. What you did this week, and the way you handled yourself, was spectacular. You showed courage, and determination, and initiative."

"And I disobeyed orders!" Stanley blurted out tearfully. "And I took a man's car and I wrecked it, and I haven't got the money to pay him for it either!"

Stanley stood looking down at his feet, sobbing uncontrollably, as Uncle Dickie drew a deep breath. "Beamish," he said sternly. "Pull yourself together man, and stop blubbering."

The room grew silent, as everyone became aware of the scene at the window.

"Now," said Uncle Dickie. "Tell me what you did."

Stanley sat on the edge of the sofa, and told Uncle Dickie everything. About catching the train, and soiling his pants, and the red sweatshirt, and taking the clothes and renting the car from the man who owned the pub in Snartley-on-Sea, and the McGregors tossing it onto the beach. "I'm sorry sir," he said, holding his head up straight. "I'm really, really sorry."

Uncle Dickie looked solemnly at Stanley, who stood and hung his head once more.

"Hmm…," the old man said. "Toss them back, boys, it looks like we have a little cleaning up to do."

The caddie wagon and Hammy's Land Rover followed the Bentley down the coast road to the spot where the Mini had tumbled down the hill. Stanley sat in the backseat, behind Uncle Dickie and the Maharajah.

"Right here, sir," he said quietly.

Uncle Dickie pulled over, followed by the boys behind, and they all clambered out to take a look. Hammy backed to the edge of the gentle drop-off to the beach, and Mills and Boon made their way down the rocky slope with a length of tow rope, which they attached to the chassis of the mini, and the electric winch on the back of Hammy's vehicle. Within minutes, the little car was back on the grass, and shortly thereafter, Mills had the engine kicking into life, and Hammy hauled it easily back to the asphalt.

"All right, then," said Uncle Dickie. "Let's go home."

Hammy threw his arms around Stanley and clapped him on the back.

"Thanks for everything, Hammy," Stanley said.

"Nae problem, Stanley," Hammy replied. "It wuz a pleasure meetin' all of you fellas, and if ye ever get up this way again, make sure ye're no strangers, okay?" He shook everyone's hand, finishing with Uncle Dickie, who slipped an arm around his shoulder.

"Well, Hamilton old boy, I must admit, I never thought I'd shake the hand of the man who carried the bag for the devil who did away with Sir Basil Strangely-Smallpiece."

Hammy looked at Uncle Dickie in amazement.

"But ah wuz just a boy," he said.

"Yes," replied Uncle Dickie. "But not so long ago, in the dungeon beneath my home, I saw a photograph of you, standing with your uncle and his golf clubs. I never forget a face, Mr. McGregor, or, for that matter, a kindness. You have my gratitude, and my friendship for life."

Hammy reddened, and looked at the rest of the men, who were looking on in amazement.

"Well, sir, that's an honor ah'll no' soon forget. God speed tae yuz all."

Hammy stood in the gathering gloom, and waved until the glow of the tail lights had vanished around the corner. He pulled a cloth cap from his jacket pocket, settled it on his head, and clambered back into the Range Rover, where he drew a huge breath, and let it out with a sigh.

"Tha' wuz a bloody day an a half, tha' wuz."

Stanley tucked in behind the other two vehicles and struggled with the steering wheel as the strange little convoy made its way south. The mini's wheel alignment had obviously been damaged, and he was hoping that nothing would come adrift on what was clearly going to be an arduous trip back to the Wood. Uncle Dickie had been ominously silent over the issue of Stanley's punishment, and had said only that Mills would repair the Mini, and it would be up to Stanley to deliver it back to its owner. Up ahead, he could hear cheers and singing coming from the caddie wagon, as the lads celebrated their momentous day. With no windows, and at fifty miles an hour, Stanley had no such warmth and, it seemed, little to be cheerful about.

CHAPTER EIGHTEEN

At the stroke of midnight, the Bentley crossed the border at Berwick-on-Tweed, and headed west on the narrow country two-lane toward Scroughtly.

A few minutes later, the light came on in the back room of the Police Station, and Finkter opened the door to let Oglesby, Mellon, and Sir Stanford in. By this time, Finkter had finished the brandy and had only two Percodan left, and his earlier feeling of indestructible euphoria had been replaced by a mood that was flickering between psychopathic violence and the giggles. He beckoned the two men to come inside and, after checking up and down the alley, he closed the door. In the kitchen, the surviving ferret was dozing in the cage on the table, and Finkter had the other one stuffed headfirst into his shirt pocket. It was now ramrod stiff, and its tail was sticking out like a bottle-brush.

Mellon put a small leather physician's bag on the floor, leaned against the refrigerator, and folded his arms. Oglesby had changed out of the battered tweed jacket and egg-stained tie that was his normal uniform, and was wearing navy blue sweat pants and a black leather jacket, while Sir Stanford was still in his suit and looking decidedly uncomfortable.

"I really don't know if I should be taking part in this," he said. "Finkter, are you sure we can get in and out without being noticed?"

Finkter sat down in the tiny kitchen, put his feet up on the table, and drawled in a really bad Bogart, "Shtan, if I washn't shure, do you think I'd be involved?" He reached into the drawer, pulled out a pack of Gauloises, and tapped one of them on the table. "I mean, you undershtand that I shtand to looshe all this, if thish little charade goes wrong, don't you?" he said, waving the cigarette around. He pulled a book of matches from his pocket, struck one, and cupped his hands over the Gauloise, lighting both it and the dead ferret simultaneously. He leaned back in the chair, and took a huge draw, as Oglesby and Sir Stanford looked on in horror. The ferret's tail started to smolder, and then suddenly ignited.

Oglesby grabbed a wet dishcloth from the sink and drove it into Finkter's chest, knocking him backward off the chair and into the stove with a clang. The ferret fell out of his pocket, and skidded across the floor toward Sir Stanford, who stamped on it several times, sending a squirt of entrails streaking up the back door.

Mellon covered his eyes and shook his head. "I can't believe I'm doing this," he said.

"Oh, oh, oh," Finkter said, as he got up slowly, feeling the back of his head. "You know, that didn't even hurt! In fact, compared to shome of the thingsh that have happened to me in the lasht couple of daysh, it wash quite pleashant!" He turned to Sir Stanford, who was looking on, slack-jawed.

Finkter suddenly grabbed his crotch and said, "Shtan, I have a little pipe in here to let the fluid out, how cool ish that?" and started to laugh. He was slapping the table, and shaking uncontrollably, with tears running down his cheeks as he said, "In fact, if you think about it, I have two!"

Mellon rummaged in his bag, and produced a pencil-thin flashlight. He held Finkter by the forehead and shone the light into his eyes, first left, then right. "Yup," he said. "He's in there all right, but for how much longer, I don't know."

Oglesby looked at Sir Stanford. "It's now or never," he said. "Come on, you take one arm, and I'll take the other. All we need is for him to show us the entrance to the tunnel."

They guided Finkter to the door, where he started to fight. He wrenched himself free and darted back to the dresser, where he grabbed a pair of wraparound sunglasses. He put them on, stuffed the remains of the charred ferret back in his pocket, and then barged out of the door in front of Oglesby. Oglesby picked up the cage and slipped out after Sir Stanford and Mellon.

Finkter had pulled his ski mask on over the sunglasses. "Follow me," he said and promptly fell over the low fence into his back garden, bursting into hysterical laughter again. Oglesby and Sir Stanford fished him out, and the strange foursome made their way up the alley to the top of the hill and down behind the main street to the entrance to Hadrian's Lane. They climbed over the stile in the wall and kept tight to the hedges that bordered the fields, and soon the whitewashed walls of the maintenance shed were glimmering a translucent, ghostly white, out of the darkness in front of them. Finkter had insisted on leading the way and as they reached the shed, he held his hand up and hissed, "Wait here, I'll check to shee if the coasht ish clear."

He tiptoed around the corner, made his way all the way around the building, and silently crept up behind the little group, as they huddled in the darkness against the wall. He put one hand against the wall, and leaned down to get as close as he possibly could to Mellon's ear, before saying, "Gotcha!" and falling down laughing again.

Mellon let out a small high-pitched shriek, and stood up quickly, head-butting Oglesby in the seat of the pants in the process, and knocking him into Sir Stanford, who fell face first into a pile of fermenting grass cuttings.

Finkter was laughing so hard now, he was choking on his swollen tongue.

Mellon, Oglesby, and Sir Stanford picked themselves up, and Mellon pounced on Finkter, straddling him, and holding him down by the throat.

"Listen, you prick!" he spat. "Just tell us where the entrance to the tunnel is, and get the hell out of here, okay?"

Finkter was slapping the cobblestones with one hand, and trying to loosen Mellon's grip on his throat with the other. "Heeere," he gasped. "It'sh right here!"

Mellon let go and looked where Finkter had pointed. A few feet to the left, there was an iron grating in the cobblestones. He clambered off Finkter and crawled over to it. "Oglesby, Stanford," he whispered. "Give us a hand with this."

They pulled the heavy cover off, staggered over to the grass verge with it, and put it down silently. By the time they got back to the vent, Finkter was gone, and the theme to the *X-Files* was floating out of the tunnel.

"Shit!" said Mellon. He grabbed his bag, pulled out the flashlight, and dropped into the tunnel. Oglesby followed with the cage, and then Sir Stanford.

Penfold Jr., the greenskeeper, was having a bad evening. Since his father's death, the responsibility for keeping the course in shape had rested solely upon him, and he seldom finished work before ten o'clock in the evening. He desperately wanted to be asleep, but his gout had been giving him hell, and he'd got to that stage in his life, where peeing a full stream was just a distant memory. He stood at the pot in his nightshirt, yawning, and digging at his backside with his left hand. He shivered violently, as he squirted out the last few pitiful drops that had awakened him. "Talk about shaking hands with the unemployed," he muttered to himself as he leaned forward to pull the handle.

He stopped suddenly and cocked his head to one side. Strange, he thought, it almost sounded like someone was whistling in the toilet. He shook his head, and flushed. Then, as he was washing his hands, he heard someone in the sink yell, "Aaaaargh!" It was muffled, he thought, but it was definitely an, "Aaaargh!" Penfold walked into the living room to check if the TV was off, and then back into the bathroom, where he stood quietly with his hands on his hips and listened.

Down in the tunnel, Finkter had just come into contact with somebody else's urine, for the third time in forty-eight hours. He was wringing out the dead ferret, when the other three came around the bend, stumbling in the dim light from Mellon's tiny flashlight. Finkter whirled around and pointed his big police-issue Halogen at the three men, blinding them.

"Look, boysh," he exclaimed, swinging the ferret by the tail. "Mine'sh gone all floppy again!"

Penfold was bending over the sink with his ear close to the

drain. Upon hearing this, he stood bolt upright, with an expression of disgust. He had heard about people like this, hanging around in public conveniences, and exposing themselves, but he couldn't believe it was going on here in Scroughtly. They must be up to something appalling, he thought, if they had to hide in a place like the tunnel to do it.

Penfold strode into the living room, picked up the telephone, and dialed the Scroughtly Police Station. Not surprisingly, there was no answer.

"Typical," Penfold said to himself, as he tried the Nerdlington Station instead. "That big twat Finkter sits on his arse all his life, and the minute you need him, he's somewhere else."

In Nerdlington, the desk sergeant on duty was Officer Winston Umbongo, a seventeen-year veteran of Zambian descent. Winston had dozed off around eleven, and was none too pleased to be aroused at this time. He lifted his head off the desk and listened disinterestedly, until Penfold got to the part about Finkter being unobtainable, which stiffened Winston up immediately. He assured Penfold that he would be there in twenty minutes, hung up, and pulled on his overcoat. Officer Umbongo had endured many of Sergeant James Finkter's racist jibes over the years, and was going to jump at any chance to discredit him. A few moments later, Winston's revolving blue light was piercing the darkness, as he sped toward Scroughtly in his brand new, navy blue police van.

Back in the greenskeepers' cottage, Penfold's next call was to the caddieshack, where he roused Herpy and Pogo. Then he dialed Gussett Hall.

Auntie Myrtle slipped the black silk eyeshades off her head and reached for the telephone. "Hello?"

She listened for a few seconds, and said, "Thank you, Penfold. No, no, you did the right thing. I'll let the Major know immediately."

Auntie Myrtle dialed quickly, and just a few miles away, Uncle Dickie's car phone trilled, waking up the Maharajah with a jolt. Uncle Dickie hit Speakerphone, and said,

"Gussett here."

"Darling, come quickly," Auntie Myrtle said. "Penfold has called the police. There's someone in the tunnel!"

"On my way, my dear!" said Uncle Dickie. "Over and out!"

The old man's lip curled upward as he sank his right foot to the floor, and the big car surged forward out of Nerdlington, and on to the straightaway toward Scroughtly. The Maharajah's turban fell backward off his head once more, as his feet came off the floor, and he clutched at the center console for balance.

"Oh, bloody hell, Dickie!" he wailed. "I'm telling you, we're getting too old for this!"

Finkter fumbled in his pocket for the remaining two Percodan. Good, he thought, they were still there. He shone his flashlight ahead. He figured he was about another hundred yards from something to wash them down with. As they fumbled on, the tunnel got progressively narrower and lower, and Oglesby noticed that Finkter was banging his big, misshapen head more often, but it didn't seem to be bothering him.

Finally, they reached the end of the tunnel, and above them, was another iron grating. Finkter reached up and pushed, and the others helped to shove it to one side. One by one, they struggled out of the hole into the space beneath the veranda steps. Sir Stanford was last out, and by this time like the rest of them, he was covered in grass slime, mud, and God knew what else from the tunnel.

Finkter was on a mission now. While the other three paused to catch their breath, he forced a couple of boards off the veranda siding and squeezed out into the night air.

Across the parking lot, Herpy and Pogo were up and keeping an eye on the clubhouse from a crack in the blinds of the caddieshack. The other three men emerged, and Mellon crept up the steps with his bag. It was too dark to make out their faces, but when Finkter stood up, there was no mistaking his tall hulking silhouette against the whitewashed boards.

"Holy shit!" said Herpy.

"What? What?" said Pogo anxiously.

Herpy rubbed the sleep from his eyes, and squinted through the crack once more. He turned to Pogo.

"It's Finkter!"

Pogo hopped over to the telephone and called Penfold, who had just heard tires on the gravel outside, and seen the headlights of Winston's van sweep across his curtains. Penfold picked up the telephone, said, "You're not serious!" and hung up. He opened his front door as Winston was walking up the garden path. "They're down at the clubhouse, four of them," he said.

Winston turned on his heel and headed back to the van.

"And one of them's Finkter!" Penfold called after him. "Winston, wait for me!"

Mellon squeezed a little lubricant onto the glass pane, put the sucker on it, and turned the diamond blade around a couple of times. Then he tapped on the glass with a small leather covered hammer, and removed the disc, which he dropped silently into his bag. He reached inside, and slid back the deadbolt. He opened the door, smiling evilly, and said, "After you, gentlemen."

Once they were inside, Mellon switched on his tiny flashlight, and pointed it at Finkter's face "Right, you big dickhead," he said. "Where do we go from here?"

Finkter grinned, and said, "You can hang on here for a moment, I'll be right back!" and tiptoed off up the corridor toward the bar, groping in his pocket for the Percodan.

"Finkter!" Sir Stanford hissed. "FINKTER, YOU MORON! Get back here!"

But it was too late, Finkter had slipped into the darkness, and was heading for the bar.

Sir Stanford was beginning to wish, and not for the first time today, that he had stayed in St. Andrews, and been content with the club collection that he had. He slid his hands down his thighs, which were thick with an indescribable ooze. There was nothing around to wipe the crud off with, either. Worse than that, the chill night air had taken its toll on his bladder, and he had been desperately needing to relieve himself for some time now.

Mellon took the lead, and set off down the hallway to find Finkter, signaling for the others to follow. They crept down the corridor, past the portrait of Sir Basil Strangely-Smallpiece and the trophy case, and Sir Stanford cheered up a little when he noticed some of the beautiful old clubs that lay behind the glass. They did not escape the attention of Oglesby either, and he turned to give Sir Stanford the thumbs up as they tiptoed into the bar, where Finkter was glugging noisily on a bottle of brandy.

Finkter gasped and put both hands on the bar, to see if that would stop the room from swirling, but it was too late. He went down with a crashing of broken glass that stopped the other three in their tracks. Mellon winced, and hunched his shoulders, waiting for some sign that they had been discovered, but all was quiet. Then, a sudden beam of light shot out from behind the bar, and started to dance around the room.

"He's got his flashlight on!" Mellon said, leaping over to the source of the light. There was a muffled, "Oof!" and the light went out.

In the brief period of illumination, however, Sir Stanford had spotted a door marked "Toilet." He left Oglesby and Mellon to deal with Finkter, and felt his way over to the door and let himself in. A little moonlight spilled inside from the high windows, and as he felt his way along the wall, he bumped against a wicker laundry basket. He delved inside, groped around, and his hands quickly came across the familiar feel of tweed, and a zipper. He couldn't resist the thought of wearing something relatively clean and dry, so he tucked the garment under his arm, quickly pulled off his trousers, and fumbled his way over to a urinal, where he relieved himself.

He was feeling much better as he opened the door to the bar, and with the dry trousers under his arm, he crept back out to see how things were going. There was just enough light from Mellon's flashlight for him to see that they had got Finkter upright, and he was slouching on the edge of a barstool. Oglesby was fiddling with the door of the ferret cage. Finkter was clearly delirious and was rummaging in the doctor's bag as Mellon tried to sit him up. He pulled out the tube of lubricant and giggled.

Sir Stanford sat down on the edge of the stool next to them, and set about putting on the trousers.

The door to the ferret cage was stuck, and Oglesby was beside himself. He tried in vain to open it, and eventually took a swing at it with his elbow, sending it skidding across the bar, and into Bertie Featherstone, who up until this point, had been sitting unnoticed at the end of the bar, minding his own business. Now, just as Finkter was coming back to life, Bertie toppled slowly forward onto the floor with a dull thud, at exactly the same time that Sir Stanford realized that he had been trying to put on one of Major Norma Oglesby's enormous tweed skirts. Sir Stanford slid off the stool and onto his hands and knees beside Bertie, just as Mellon lost his grip on Finkter.

Finkter was standing up and staggering over Sir Stanford, with the tube of lubricant in one hand and the wet ferret dangling from the other, when the door to the bar burst open, and Winston Umbongo switched on the lights. Pogo, Herpy, and Penfold craned over his shoulders to get a look.

Finkter spun around, and shouted, "Winshton!"

Then he looked at the ferret dangling in his right hand.

"Don't worry," he grinned. "We have one that ishn't dead yet!"

Penfold pointed and slapped Winston on the shoulder. "You see!" he said excitedly. "I told you they were perverts!" He produced a small disposable camera, and Sir Stanford held up his hand and winced, as the flash bulb popped. Finkter was the only one of the four that managed a smile.

For Winston Umbongo, it seemed that Kwanzaa, or Chanukah, or whatever, had come early and all at once. Then there was a loud screech of tires from outside, and the window to the bar was peppered with gravel. A few seconds later, Uncle Dickie skidded into the room, followed by the Maharajah. He cast his eye over the scene and grinned broadly.

"I say, Stanford!" he said enthusiastically. "How awfully nice to see you!"

As the caddie wagon and the little red mini trundled into the parking lot, the flashing blue light on Winston's van gave the boys their first clue that something was going on. The parking-lot floodlights were on, and Winston was helping a handcuffed Sir Stanford into the back of the van, where Mellon, Oglesby, and Finkter were already sitting. Sir Stanford was protesting loudly, Oglesby was sniveling, and Finkter had his head in Mellon's lap, singing, "We are the Champions, my friend," at the top of his voice.

Stanley shivered violently, as he eased himself stiffly out of the mini and joined the small huddle of people around the van, as the door of Flanagan's cottage burst open, and Agnes ran

out, followed by Auntie Myrtle.

"Ooh, dear God," Agnes yelled, running toward Flanagan, her arms outstretched. "Ah've bin so worried!"

Flanagan was about to open his mouth, when Dwilby shot between his legs, sprang into Agnes's arms, and began to lick her face.

"Aye," Flanagan said. "Tha's about right."

Uncle Dickie clapped him on the back.

"Never mind, Flanagan, old boy," he said. "You have to admit, he was the hero of the day."

Uncle Dickie turned to Auntie Myrtle and hugged her, lifting her feet off the ground. She ran her hands across his battered face and frowned.

"That's it," she said sternly. "No more of this nonsense for you, Gussett. You're too old for fighting, and that's that."

Uncle Dickie smiled at her and reached into the backseat of the Bentley. He pulled out the ancient wooden box and handed it to her.

"Some things are worth fighting for, my dear," he said.

Auntie Myrtle shook her head, and turned to Agnes.

"Did you hear that Agnes?" she said loudly. "Some things are worth fighting for, like this, apparently."

Agnes put Dwilby down and patted him on the head. "Lucky they had this wee man on their side then," she said with a smile.

Aunt Myrtle opened the box and took out the digit. "You're quite right," she said. "The hero deserves a treat." Then, to Uncle Dickie's horror, she tossed the Digit to Dwilby, who caught it neatly, chewed it a couple of times, and then swallowed with a gulp.

"AAARGH!" screamed Uncle Dickie. "Bloody Hell, Myrtle, what did you just do?" He held his head in his hands, and stared at her in disbelief. "That was the oldest trophy in all of sport!" He staggered forward toward Dwilby, with his arms outstretched.

Auntie Myrtle rolled her eyes, and shook her head at him.

"No it wasn't, you old goat," she said. "It was a piece of beef jerky."

Uncle Dickie stopped in his tracks, and looked at her quizzically.

"Excuse me?"

"Heavens, Dickie," Auntie Myrtle said. "You didn't think I'd let McGregor steal the real one, did you? I had Wilberforce, your taxidermist, carve a replica from a piece of dried wildebeest."

Uncle Dickie's mouth hung open, as he pointed a finger at her, and nodded his head dumbly. The weight of the day had finally hit him, and in his weakened state, this was too much for him to comprehend. Flanagan stepped in behind him as he fainted, and lowered him gently to the ground.

Aunt Myrtle pursed her lips and whistled softly. "That's my soldier, Agnes," she said. Then she turned to the Maharajah, who was also looking more than a little dumbstruck.

"What?" she said. "Somebody has to run things around here, Poony. Heaven knows, all of you are too busy playing games. I just hope I can get back to my gardening now, that's all. Stanley, take the Major over to the Dormy House and put him to bed, there's a good fellow."

Then Auntie Myrtle clapped her hands, and said, "Right everyone, it's time for bed."

Winston slammed the door of the police van, turned off his blue light, and headed for Nerdlington, and the little crowd dissolved, leaving Stanley and Flanagan, who heaved Uncle Dickie into a sitting position as Thirsty popped open the trunk of the Bentley to get the bags.

He froze and turned to Flanagan and Stanley, who had Uncle Dickie's arms draped around their necks.

"What?" said Flanagan.

"The clubs," Thirsty said, swallowing hard. "They're gone!"

Uncle Dickie twitched suddenly and opened one eye, which bored into Thirsty.

"The Bungley wedge," he wheezed. "Is it there?"

Thirsty bent over into the trunk and groped around for a moment. He emerged slowly, swallowed once more, and said quietly, "No, sir."

With an enormous effort Uncle Dickie raised his head and, for a moment, Stanley thought he saw a flicker of a smile.

It was barely audible, but all three men heard him croak,

"Excellent."